THE EAGLE STONE

While assisting her father in selling provisions to visitors to the top of Snowdon, Elinor Owen meets the adventuress Lady Sara Raglan and her handsome nephew, Richard. Eli is swiftly drawn into Lady Sara's most recent adventure, becoming a spy for Queen Victoria's government. Now, up against the evil Jacques, Eli and Richard are soon fighting for their lives, while Lady Sara heads for a final showdown and pistols at dawn with Jacques on the summit of Snowdon itself.

Books by Heather Pardoe
in the Linford Romance Library:

HER SECRET GARDEN
THE IVORY PRINCESS
THE SOARING HEART

HEATHER PARDOE

THE EAGLE STONE

Complete and Unabridged

LINFORD
Leicester

First published in Great Britain in 2006

First Linford Edition
published 2007

British Library CIP Data

Pardoe, Heather
    The eagle stone.—Large print ed.—
Linford romance library
    1. Snowdon (Wales)—Fiction
    2. Romantic suspense novels
    3. Large type books
    I. Title
    823.9'2 [F]

ISBN 978–1–84617–607–4

Published by
F. A. Thorpe (Publishing)
Anstey, Leicestershire

Set by Words & Graphics Ltd.
Anstey, Leicestershire
Printed and bound in Great Britain by
T. J. International Ltd., Padstow, Cornwall

1

A cold wind swirled round the mountain tops and flung itself with a shower of hailstones into the faces of the two figures on the narrow path just below Mount Snowdon's summit.

'You all right there, are you, Eli?' Daniel Owen demanded, looking back to where his daughter had come to a sudden stop behind him, turning her head away from the harsh blast and pulling her bonnet closer around her head.

'Yes, Dad, don't worry,' Elinor replied as the shower faded away.

She turned back to smile at him, the pale oval of her face beneath the sodden material of her bonnet brightened by the glow of her cheeks which had been burnished bright red by the cold wind and the effort of their long climb.

'Me and Blod, here, we're used to this in all weathers,' Daniel said, patting the flank of the heavily-laden donkey waiting by his side, chewing gloomily at some imaginary piece of vegetation.

Up here was as high as you could get in all of England and Wales, so Eli had been reminded frequently at school, and only bare rock could be seen on either side of the rough path, so poor Blod would have to resign herself to not a single blade of fresh grass until they made their way down towards the village that evening.

'Not that it will last,' Daniel added, rubbing his frozen hands together. 'It's already clear over the sea. A fine day it will be once that sun gets up, and plenty of customers for us.'

'Yes, Dad,' she murmured in reply.

At this moment, she couldn't care if the sun rose or not. Her feet ached, her legs ached, even her shoulders ached, from the small pack strung across her back. The hem of her skirt was heavy with mud and water, while her petticoats were not fit to be seen, and she could feel a small trickle of cold making its way down her back where a hailstone had found its way beneath the collar of her coat.

All she wanted to do was stop, crawl into any hole she could find, and go to sleep.

'Drat all customers,' she muttered beneath her breath.

Who on earth, she asked herself, not for the first time, would choose to climb mountains for fun? The moment Howel's leg mended and he was able to return to helping their dad through wind and weather he was welcome to it, and she would never, never complain ever again that serving behind the counter at Mrs Hughes' bakery in Llanberis was tedious. It was warm and dry, and you weren't likely to be blown over cliff-edges at any moment, never to be seen again.

'Not long now. Just this last steep bit, and we're there.'

'Good.'

'You're doing well, Eli, this being you're first time up so high. We'll soon have you up here fast as a mountain goat.'

'Over my dead body,' she muttered into her scarf as she wound it back round as much of her face as she could cover, and hitched up her sodden skirts in preparation for setting off once more.

Dad chuckled.

'It's not so bad. They'll be having a railway up here in no time. Then we can travel up in style.'

'A railway?'

Eli stared. A railway, up here? She looked down into the valley behind them, every route as steep as could be. How could anyone even think of getting such a thing up here?

They'd been up the coast on a train last summer, all the way up to Conwy to see Aunt Mair who lived in a tiny cottage just beneath the castle walls. Eli had never imagined there could be anything that made so much noise, and let out enough steam for the odd dragon or so to boast of, as the shiny black engine that pulled the smart, new carriages fast enough to take her breath away. Twenty miles an hour at least, so Dad said.

The railways had reached the North Wales coast when Dad was a boy. He had watched them, the teams of men digging out the embankments and the tunnels and laying the tracks for the new-fangled machines to pass over.

'There's been talk of a railway up to the summit of Snowdon for years,' Daniel continued, setting Blod on her way up the path once more. 'Soon as old Assheton Smith can be persuaded to sell some of his land, and Beddgelert and Llanberis can decide which village of the two the train goes up from, there'll be a railway up here, just you see.'

'More customers for us, then,' Eli said brightly.

'The end of the business, more like. I can bet you every large hotel in Llanberis has their eyes on a piece of Snowdon's summit. Small businesses like ours won't stand a chance.'

'But that's not fair, Dad. You said the Owens had a hut up here for years and years, before most of those hotels were even built.'

'You'll soon find there's nothing fair in this world where money is concerned, my dear. That's why I'm telling you and Howel not to put your heart into the business. Why else do you think I've been sending Howel out with the guides to learn the routes to take the visitors in summer? And you must keep working at your studying, and teaching at the Sunday school for the chapel.'

He stopped and gazed at her earnestly.

'It's a good mind you've got in that head of yours, Elinor, and you don't want to be working for Mrs Hughes for ever. We'll make a teacher of you yet. So don't you go marrying any farmer's son in a hurry. A hard life a farmer's wife has of it, I can tell you that. I'm a farmer's son. You can do better than that.'

'Yes, Dad,' she replied.

Well, at least Dad wasn't worrying about her failure to find any serious suitor, she reflected. She'd be twenty-two next birthday, and most girls of her age in the village were already married with a baby or two at their heels. It wasn't that there weren't any young men interested . . . Griff Griffiths, for instance. He'd been pressing her for an answer again only yesterday. Eli shivered.

Even Dad might say Griff was an enviable match for a village girl, his dad being head gardener for the Penrhyns in their castle by the coast at Bangor, and Griff all ready to step into his father's footsteps. But there was something about Griff. Eli frowned, puzzling it over. She should be mad, thinking of turning down an offer of a beautiful new house on Lord Penrhyn's estate, and a settled existence for life. There would certainly be no getting up with the dawn to milk the cattle, and trudging through the snow in search of lost sheep on the hillsides. Compared to most girls in the village she would be marrying into a life of ease and riches. And yet there was something about Griff . . .

In front of her, Dad had stopped. He was pushing back his hood and looking around him with the expression of a man well satisfied with life.

'Now that's what I call a view,' he remarked.

Eli pulled herself out of her reflections and took the few steps up to join him. Griff Griffiths flew out of her head along with the wind tugging at her bonnet. They had reached the very top of the mountain at last. On one side, the rugged cliffs of Snowdon curved round into its horseshoe shape, with the glint of the lake caught in the middle. Across those slate-green waters, so the story went, King Arthur had been rowed to his last resting place amongst the cliffs of the horseshoe, to wait until Wales needed him again. On every side, smaller peaks stretched out into the distance as far as she could see, broken only by the distant blue of the sea.

'It's like being on the top of the world!' she exclaimed.

The cloud was clearing, but one or two wisps floated by below them. All of a sudden, she had forgotten the cold and the wet and the aching of her limbs, and was standing there entranced by the sight of more of the earth than she had ever hoped to see in her entire life stretched out below her.

'Now you see what I mean.' Dad grinned. 'It's always the same feeling, however often you come up here. It's always different, see. And here we are, the only people up so high.'

'Not for long,' Eli replied, peering down into the horseshoe, her attention caught by a slight movement below. 'Look, down on the path by the lake, there's a party making its way up.'

'Gosh, they're eager, then. Must have stayed in Capel Curig to be starting out so early.'

'Looks like four of them,' Eli said.

'The one at the front will be the guide, unless they are really foolish,' he remarked. 'I've known visitors to come up without. Usually one of these plant collectors, after some fern or other and worried someone will find the site and take the lot.' He gave a grim chuckle. 'And many a one I've helped in the rescuing when they get lost or twist an ankle, I can tell you. Now who could be so foolish as to give their life for a few leaves, eh?'

He turned back to the donkey.

'Come on then, Blod, time to get to work, old girl. They'll be wanting a cup of tea and a warm place to sit by the time they make their way up here.'

He peered down towards his prospective customers with an expert eye.

'Aye, aye,' he added, a note of disapproval creeping in, 'and two of them women, at that.'

'Really?'

Eli looked more closely. As a long stretch of cloud moved away from in front of her she could make out the unmistakeable shapes of long skirts and bonnets swathed around two of the distant figures.

'I didn't know there were many women who climbed up here.'

'There didn't used to be,' Daniel said, his disapproval deepening. 'At least not many, but now, with these new-fangled ideas of women taking up sports, they're coming up by the dozen. There was even one last year came up bold as brass in just her — yes, well.'

He cleared his throat, meeting his daughter's wide-eyed gaze with an embarrassed look.

'And don't let that be giving you ideas, mind. I didn't know where to look.'

'It might be more practical without all these petticoats,' Eli said.

She had heard rumours of women riding bicycles in just their bloomers, without a skirt to be seen, some even daring to wear trousers, like a man. Mind you, she wasn't about to tell Dad how much she relished the prospect of being freed from her cumbersome skirts.

She looked down at the approaching climbers with a growing sense of excitement. These visitors really did come from a different world, she could feel it — a world beyond the mountains, where women travelled and climbed mountains, and maybe even rode bicycles in just their bloomers. Eli suddenly felt energy flooding through her. She would not have missed this day for all the world.

'Hurry up there, Elinor,' Dad was calling.

He had already reached a small hut, created out of stones, and protected from the worst of the wind in a dip in the ridge, and was unloading provisions from Blod's unprotesting back.

'We've work to be done if that tea is to be hot when they get here.'

'Coming!' Elinor called brightly.

With one last look down at the visitors, bringing a scarcely-to-be-imagined world of possibilities in their every step, she turned and made her way down from the summit to join him.

2

Just a few more steps, Aunt Sara. Take your time now, as we're almost there.'

At the sound of the man's voice, Eli paused in her mission to unload the last of Mam's cakes from Blod's panniers to watch the visitors arrive at the summit, her curiosity screened from view by the donkey's broad flanks. The guide had already reached the summit, while the younger man behind him had turned to help the elder of his two companions over the last few stones.

'I can manage well enough, thank you, Richard,' the sharp reply came.

Elinor grinned as a tall, angular woman, with a mass of grey hair escaping from beneath her bonnet, brushed her nephew's hand impatiently aside.

'I'm not an invalid yet.'

'I wouldn't dare suggest it, Aunt.'

Eli could hear the suppressed laughter in his voice. It was a warm voice, she decided, pausing rather longer than she had intended, warm and understanding, not the kind of man to stand on his dignity. She attempted to take a clearer look, but his face was turned away towards the second woman, a much younger woman — a remarkably pretty young woman, Eli noted with an unexpected sense of gloom. Not that he was likely to even notice her, she thought, and even if he did, where on earth were they ever likely to meet again?

'I take it you are also in no need of assistance,' he remarked.

The newcomer laughed. A warm, charming laugh, Eli noted, her gloom deepening, not the kind you could imagine disliking at all.

'Don't you even dare,' she retorted. 'Didn't you see we were only holding back to save your pride, Richard? Aunt Sara could have outstripped you at any time.'

'Then the next climb we make I'll demand that you prove it,' he answered, laughing.

'And I'll take you up on it. Prepare for total humiliation, Richard.'

Their voices faded into an indistinguishable murmur as they turned away from Eli's hiding place to admire the view.

'Eli? Not lost out there, are you?'

'No, Dad, I'm just coming.'

Hastily she unstrapped the basket of cakes and took them back inside the hut.

'You were right,' she remarked. 'The weather is brightening already, and the first visitors have arrived.'

'Good, good. This water is just about boiling in time then.'

Inside the little hut it was dark, but with the blaze of the fire, and sheltered from the wind, it seemed delightfully warm after the freezing wind of their climb. As she busied herself unwrapping the cakes and placing them appealingly on view on a slate shelf propped up on stones near the entrance to the hut, Eli could feel the warmth flooding through her, while steam rose gently from the soaked hem of her skirts.

She unwrapped her scarf from her face, and smoothed as much of her chestnut hair as she could find back into the confines of her bonnet. A shadow darkening the entrance of the hut had her glancing up quickly, but it was only the guide, who had left his charges admiring the view and had made his way in out of the wind.

' 'Morning, Dan,' he called. 'Nearly beat you this time.'

' 'Morning, Gwyn. Elinor spotted you on the way up. Professional climbers, is it?'

'No, no. Two English visitors, all the way from London.'

'There's posh you are today, then, Gwyn,' Daniel returned with a grin. 'Surprised you're talking to us, man.'

Gwyn Jones was a short, stockily-built man with a good-humoured round face made even rounder by a gently-receding hairline. He and Daniel had been friends since boyhood, and Elinor was quite used to the to and fro of their banter.

'You don't know the half of it, Dan,' Gwyn replied with a smile. 'You'll never guess who my third can be.'

'Don't tell me, Queen Victoria herself, or is it Miss Florence Nightingale come to build a hospital in the wilderness?'

'You're near enough. Lady Sara Raglan from the big hall, that's who.'

Daniel whistled, impressed.

'Why, she must be fifty, if she's a day.'

'Not so as you'd notice,' Gwyn returned, a trifle ruefully. 'She was up before all of us this morning, and set a fine pace, I can tell you. Claimed there wasn't a day she'd missed the mountains in all these years.'

'I should think not, living in a tent in a desert with a collection of savages,' Dad said, disapproval entering his voice again. 'I'm surprised she came back here at all, not after — '

His eyes caught his daughter's gaze of undisguised curiosity, and cleared his throat.

'Yes, well,' he muttered, gruffly.

'No choice, so they were saying in the papers,' Gwyn remarked. 'Civil war, that's what. Made the whole of the kingdom of Milat impossible. Looters, rioters, you know, that sort of thing. Those who got out were the lucky ones, so they say. Had to leave everything to get clean away. And I'm not sure she really was living in a tent, not then, at least, not in Milat. Mountainous country, so I've heard. Too cold for tents by half.'

He turned to warm his hands by the fire.

'That your mam's Bara Brith, is it, Elinor?' he added thoughtfully, eyeing the slab of moist fruit bread on the shelf next to him.

'Yes, it is. Please, do have some, Mr Jones,' Eli replied quickly, rather hoping such fuel might encourage him to carry on with his story.

She had heard of Lady Sara Raglan, of course. There was scarcely a month went by when there was not something about the latest exploit of the famous adventuress, accompanied by photographs of her riding a camel across desert sands, or climbing pyramids, or even slashing her way through some jungle or other. Several times the headlines, **Lady Raglan lost, feared dead**, had appeared along with lurid details of cannibals and pirates in the particular region in which she had last been seen.

Their greatest excitement had been last year when she had reportedly been held captive by some mountain tribe who demanded a king's ransom for her release. Lady Sara had made her way down from the mountains and through thick jungle to safety, amidst wild stories of her shooting her way out of captivity and taking one of her captors' dugout canoes to race down the local rapids to freedom.

Eli still had a copy of that last report, along with a thrilling drawing of a wide-eyed woman, one hand clenched heroically to her chest, the other waving an oar recklessly in the air. **For Queen and Country**, the caption had read, and this same woman was now standing only a few paces away from her, and might even soon be drinking Dad's tea and eating Mam's Bara Brith! Eli felt her cheeks begin to glow once more.

'Wonderful. Nothing beats your mam's Bara Brith,' Gwyn said, munching away.

'Is Lady Raglan back at the hall, then?' Eli prompted.

'Seems so. My cousin, Guto, works in the gardens there. He says she's been ordering all kinds of things. New vegetables in the kitchen garden, and all the greenhouses to be repaired. Now you don't do that unless you're planning to stay.'

'It must be good to have someone living there,' Eli said, as Mr Jones sank into an appreciative silence, licking his fingers and eyeing the rest of the Bara Brith in a thoughtful manner.

'It is, it is. Not much work around the place since the old man died. Shocking waste, big place like that going empty for so long. Shocking waste.'

'Do have another piece, Mr Jones.'

'Why, thank you, Elinor, and my compliments to your mam. This is the best I've tasted yet.'

'I'm sure she will be pleased, Mr Jones.' Eli smiled at him. 'A surprise, was it then, Lady Raglan coming back to live there?'

'Surprise? You can say that again. None of us would have taken bets on old Raglan leaving the house to her, daughter or no daughter. Not after that business with the sheik.'

'Really?' Eli said, rather too eagerly.

She saw her father frown and shake his head.

'But then, a bit thin on the ground are the Raglans,' Gwyn was continuing, 'and half of them that's left haven't spoken to the other half in years. Probably the best of a bad job as far as the old man was concerned.'

Eli poured another cup of tea. She was longing to ask about the business with the sheik, but from the expression on her father's face, she had a feeling that at the first sign of a question she would be banished outside away from any such unsuitable excitement.

Not that it was likely to give her any ideas, she reflected wryly. Sheiks might abound in the kind of novels Dad would never have allowed her to borrow from the public lending library, but they were pretty much non-existent in the rainswept wilderness of Snowdon.

'Perhaps Lady Raglan and her companions might care for tea,' Eli suggested, a little hesitantly.

'Indeed. They'll be down in a moment. Just admiring the view, so they were, when I came to see if you were all set up yet.'

There was a rush of stones outside, followed by a heavy thud and a man's voice muttering a string of curses.

'Ah, now that must be them.'

Gwyn was now settled down comfortably by the fire, deep into his second mug of strong tea, and with little sign of wishing to move again.

'I'll show them in, shall I?' Eli said, and Gwyn smiled.

'There's a good girl, you are,' he replied, stretching his feet nearer to the flames. 'Tell them there's a good fire, and enough room for us all at a pinch.'

Quick as a flash, and certainly before Dad could make any protest, Eli shot outside. There, just beyond the entrance to the small hut, a man was pulling himself up awkwardly from the ground, where he had landed amongst a group of rocks, still muttering to himself. There was no sign of his companions.

Eli stepped forward to ask if he needed any assistance. It was easy to slip on the rocks or the small scree of pebbles in between, and the matter of just one careless moment to twist an ankle, or even break a bone.

At the sound of her footsteps he swung around, almost unbalancing himself again.

'Hell and damnation,' he muttered irritably. 'D'you have to sneak up on a man like that?'

Eli blinked, the offer of assistance dying on her lips. The warm voice of earlier had built a picture in her mind, and it was not the one of the narrow-faced man with a deep scar slashed deep into one cheek, leaving a white line in the swarthy darkness of his skin, rising unsteadily to his feet before her. Her silence seemed to irritate him further.

'Dammit!' he snapped. 'Doesn't anyone in this god-forsaken country speak any English?'

He swung back to the path behind him.

'Perhaps you can understand her, Phillips,' he added.

Eli blinked again. This time there was no mistake. She had seen the young woman who had accompanied Lady

Sara with her own eyes, and the wizened, little man overburdened with a very large knapsack making his way down towards them was certainly nothing like her.

'After all, that's what I'm paying you for.'

Suddenly uneasy, Eli stepped back towards the safety of the hut. The contempt in the speaker's voice was plain for all to hear. She'd met men like that in the village. It didn't matter where they came from or what language they spoke, a strong instinct told her to keep out of their way as much as possible. They were the kind of men who used others, so Mam would say, and didn't even think of the consequences.

She took another step back, keeping her dignity for as long as she could, but instead of the softness of the blanket across the entrance, she felt herself hit hard against the solid warmth of a human body.

'Oh!' she gasped, frozen in her tracks.

Did this unpleasant stranger have an entire gang of lackeys to jump to his every bidding? She felt a large strong hand placed on her shoulder.

'Not to worry.'

Now that was the voice she had heard on the summit, warm and good-humoured. Not quite so good-humoured at the moment, though, laced, rather, with a touch of anger.

'Do I take it you make it your life's study, sir, to insult and terrorise young women?' he was demanding coldly.

She wanted to turn, steal just one glance at her knight, if not in shining armour, a good strong pair of walking boots with a stout stick, but pride kept her eyes on the narrow-faced man in front of her. He was clearly furious at this interruption. He dusted the lichen and mud from his trousers, and picked up his own stick from where it had fallen during his tumble.

'And do you always interfere with matters that do not concern you?'

'Uncalled-for bullying will always

concern me, as I hope it would any decent man,' Eli's champion replied tartly.

The narrow-faced man went pale under his sunburn.

'How dare you!' he exclaimed, but he was interrupted by a shout from the direction of the summit. Making her way rapidly towards them, skirts flying, bonnet flapping from its strings behind her, and her grey hair swirling round her head like a demon, came the figure of Sara Raglan.

'Richard, just what are you doing? Have you no respect for this place? Picking a quarrel on the very top of Snowdon is not how I expected any nephew of mine to behave. And as for you, sir!'

She rounded on Richard's opponent. Eli waited in awe and admiration for a flood of furious anger to spill out, but none came. Instead, Lady Sara pulled her bonnet back over her head and tied it into place in silence. From the corner of her eye, Eli could see that her hands were shaking.

'Well, and good morning to you, too, Sara,' the narrow-faced man said, with a less than pleasant version of a smile. 'And may I say how very honoured I am to meet you here.'

3

Such an extraordinary coincidence,' the narrow-faced man continued smoothly to which Lady Raglan snorted loudly.

'Coincidence my foot, Jacques! Just how many people did you have to bribe to find me?'

'My dear lady, if you don't wish humble visitors to your so-beautiful house to know where you are, you should instruct your housekeeper rather better.'

'Visitors are welcome to know my whereabouts. I was not expecting vermin. I had them poison the rats last week.'

Jacques clicked his tongue reprovingly.

'And such a greeting for an old friend,' he complained.

'I do not count traitors among my friends,' she retorted.

'My dear lady — '

'Or thieves and murderers, either,' she interrupted.

'Mere propaganda, I assure you.'

There was a moment's silence.

'Aunt Sara?'

Caught in this exchange, none of them had noticed the last member of Lady Raglan's party joining them. Eli felt the hand removed from her shoulder. She repressed a sigh. Well, she could hardly beg him to keep it there, and the young lady was even prettier close-to than she was from a distance.

'Aunt Sara, is everything all right?'

'Charming.'

Jacques stepped forward, reaching out to take the newcomer's hand.

'Delighted to make the acquaintance of the niece of Lady Sara,' he murmured, but his hand was knocked away smartly from its object by a flick of Lady Sara's walking stick.

'Keep your grubby paws to yourself, Jacques. Your business is with me, no-one else.'

'Business, Aunt Sara?' Richard asked.

Eli at last risked a quick glance over her shoulder at his face. Brown eyes under clearly-marked brows and a mass of dark hair. Even frowning it was the kind of face you'd turn and look at again if you passed it in the street. Eli tore her glance away, and concentrated instead on Lady Raglan.

'This gentleman,' Sara spat out the word contemptuously, 'believes I have something he is looking for.'

'Something worth climbing Snowdon to find, Aunt?' Richard said incredulously.

'Something worth keeping me in his sight, except he is wasting his time. I was searched thoroughly on numerous occasions on my way to the border. Most undignified. He is lucky I didn't cause a stir and a diplomatic incident.'

'But then, Lady Raglan can be so — well, shall we say — forceful. Maybe the searching was not always as thorough as you suggest.'

'I can assure you, Jacques, it was. If

you think there is any way I could have spirited away the Eagle Stone, then you are very much mistaken.'

'The Eagle Stone?' her niece demanded, eyes sparkling with excitement.

'A mere trifle.'

Jacques smiled, but the way his dark eyes fixed themselves on Sara as if they never intended to let go told another story.

'I take it you intend to follow me until you are certain I do not have the stone?'

'I wish to spend as much of my time here in the company of such an interesting acquaintance.'

'I'm surprised you haven't taken the opportunity to search my house,' she retorted, and Jacques smiled. 'I see. I take it you have someone undertaking the task at this moment?'

'My dear Sara, I have certain instructions. Unless I can put you in the clear, life could become very unpleasant for you.' He glanced towards her niece. 'And, sadly, for your family also.

So, you see, I really am your friend.'

'Is that a threat?' Richard asked, dangerously quietly.

'From me? No. As I said, I am here to help you.'

Sara Raglan sighed and a look of defeat settled on her features.

'Then it seems we shall not be rid of you for some time,' she remarked. 'Though what exactly you expect me to do up here, I really cannot imagine, unless you are expecting me to throw your precious stone into the lake.'

'You would not be so foolish. But there are caves here, are there not, where precious things are hidden. I was told all about them in the village. Such a good hiding place.'

'Oh, an excellent hiding place, Jacques,' Sara said with a chuckle. 'There, amongst the treasures of King Arthur, ready to be woken whenever the horn is sounded and the enemies of my country need defeating.'

Jacques frowned at her. 'It's a story, you fool. A legend.'

She burst out into laughter.

'Is that what you thought I was doing up here? If I could find the cave of King Arthur I would have no need of your Eagle Stone. It's over there, on the flanks of that ridge of the Snowdon horseshoe, should you care to look, though I should warn you, no-one has found it yet. As for me, I'm going straight back down the way we came. You wouldn't catch me falling for a children's fairytale such as that.'

Jacques eyed her with a scowl, as if undecided whether to believe her or not.

'Then I shall see you on your way,' he said at last, with an ill-tempered show of gallantry. 'This is a desolate place for ladies to be lost.'

'I've been in far worse, as well you know,' Sara replied. 'And I know every part of this mountain like the back of my hand. I was always up and down here when I was young. Mountains do not change with time, unlike people,' she added, sharply. 'Now go away,

Jacques, and let us enjoy our breakfast in peace. My only intention at this moment is to purchase a cup of tea from the hut here. Perhaps I can get one for you and your friend as well.'

The wizened man looked up hopefully at this, but Jacques merely shuddered.

'A drink?' he said, outraged. 'From such savages as these?'

Eli clenched her fist, but managed to keep her face a blank. Attracting any kind of notice from such a man had no wisdom in it, she sensed, however many insults fell from his lips. Better, much better, that her existence never registered in his mind. She kept her eyes firmly on the ground.

'You risk your stomach and your life as you choose, Lady Raglan,' he was continuing, haughtily. 'I have come better prepared.'

'I suppose I can't possibly have the pleasure of hoping this is the last time we shall ever meet.'

'Alas, no, dear lady. As I have said,

that particular matter lies in your own hands.'

'Or not, since I do not have the stone, and you are wasting your time.'

Jacques grunted.

'About that, we shall see,' he replied. 'So I shall bid you au revoir, Sara.'

'And I shall wish you goodbye,' she shot back.

With a small, ironic bow he left, his unfortunate guide staggering along behind under his load.

'What an unpleasant man,' Lady Sara's niece murmured as they watched him go.

Richard was at Sara's side in a moment, dark brows locked together in a deep frown.

'Aunt, are you quite sure this has nothing to do with you? This stone he mentioned.'

Sara patted his cheek affectionately.

'Now don't you worry about it, Richard, dear. The man is obviously clutching at straws. His masters must have misplaced the Eagle Stone in their rush to overthrow their king, and are desperate to find it. Perhaps if they claim the eccentric Lady Raglan has taken it they can put the blame for its loss on Queen Victoria, though given the size of the army she commands I do not consider this to be a wise move on their part. The Eagle Stone is worth a king's ransom in money, but it is even more precious than that. You see, without it, no coronation of a King of Milat can take place.'

'So those loyal to the deposed king would have every reason to make it disappear,' Richard said slowly.

'That is correct, dear.'

'And can you honestly say, Aunt, that if you had been asked to spirit it away you would have refused?'

'If I had been asked,' she replied with a smile, 'but I wasn't, and fond as I am of that unfortunate man, there is nothing I could do to help him.'

'Are you quite sure?' he demanded.

'Now, would I lie to you, Richard?' she replied.

Eli suppressed a grin. From the look on Richard's face, he was not at all convinced Sara was telling the truth, but as a gentleman he could hardly accuse a lady of lying. She saw a brief struggle in his features, and signs of a decision made.

'No, of course not, Aunt,' he replied.

'Good, now you take Catherine inside and get yourselves a good hot cup of tea. My father always used to say the Owens made the best tea on Snowdon.'

As Catherine ducked under the blanket, Eli made to follow her, but discovered a hand placed firmly on her arm.

'Not you, young lady,' Lady Sara was saying to her in Welsh. 'I want a word with you first.'

She turned back to her nephew and slipped back into English.

'I'll just be a moment, Richard. I've a little trouble with these old boots of mine. Go and look after your sister. This young woman is clearly an experienced mountaineer and quite the best person to help me. And if you think,' she added as he began to protest, 'that I am revealing so much as an ankle to those men in there you have another think coming. It is quite sheltered here, and we shall do well enough.'

Eli found his eyes watching her closely. She smiled, faintly, feeling rather foolish, torn between the rather delicious news that Richard's beautiful young lady companion was his sister, and the fact that he had at last noticed her own existence, but with a frown that clearly showed him to suspect her of being a hired assassin at worst, a complete idiot at least. Eli could not help a sigh as she saw the idiot part had won.

'As you wish, Aunt Sara,' he said, ducking under the blanket and vanishing into the hut.

There was a moment's silence.

'Come over here,' Lady Raglan said abruptly, marching over to a rock as far away as they could go from the hut entrance without finding themselves back in the worst of the wind. She was speaking in Welsh again. Eli did likewise.

'Can I help you?' she asked, as the older woman sat down and began to unlace her boot.

'No, no. Nothing wrong with these. Never given me a day's trouble from the moment they were made.'

She finished unlacing the boot and rested her foot on a convenient stone.

'Bit of local camouflage, that's all.'

'Oh,' Eli said, her heart suddenly beating fast inside her.

Lady Raglan straightened up and looked at her with a keen gaze from her blue eyes.

'I take it you understood everything of that?' she demanded.

Eli eyed her warily, not quite sure how to reply. This Eagle Stone was clearly a secret. A huge, dangerous secret, from everything that had passed between Jacques and the woman in front of her. Was Lady Raglan afraid she couldn't keep her mouth shut and was about to let the entire village know within the hour of Dad and her returning?

She swallowed. Lady Raglan was rich and powerful. If she wanted the Owen family removed from the area they would find themselves on the next train to London and a one-way ticket to the uncertainties of making a new life in a far-away town.

'Of what?' she ventured, keeping her face as blank as she was able.

To her surprise Lady Raglan laughed out loud.

'Clever girl,' she said approvingly. 'I was watching you, young woman. You never missed a thing, and yet you looked for all the world as if you couldn't follow a word. I've met spies who couldn't control their faces as you do, and well paid by governments they were, too.'

'I'm not a spy!' Eli protested, alarmed.

'I know you're not, but you are clever, and you can think fast on your feet. It may be that I shall have need of someone like you.'

Eli blinked.

'You mean, the Eagle Stone?'

'Don't ask. Don't even think,' Lady Raglan said sharply. 'The less you know, the better. Jacques would never have mentioned the thing unless he was quite certain you could not understand him. He is clever, but not clever enough to gain local knowledge, not at least the kind that counts. If he had lowered himself to take the trouble he might have known that Daniel Owen who runs the hut up here married an Englishwoman, and the chances are that you are their daughter. I am right, I take it?'

Eli grinned.

'Yes,' she said. 'My mother comes from Birmingham.'

'Yes, I thought I remembered that. So your English is as good as mine.'

'Not as good I'm sure, Lady Raglan.'

'No false modesty, Miss Owen. If I remember rightly, Dan was a clever young man, and more than usually enthusiastic about education. I take it you can read and write?'

'Yes, Lady Raglan.'

'And just how long do you intend to work for your father, trailing up Snowdon every day?'

'I don't usually,' Eli said, her heart taking off again at an extraordinary pace. 'My brother usually helps Dad, but he broke his leg, so I'm helping him until it heals. My usual work is at Mrs Hughes' bakery in Llanberis.'

'And from your tone, I take it you would not mind if you never returned there.'

Eli took a deep breath. Only a few hours ago, she would have given everything she ever owned to be back in Mrs Hughes' bakery. At this moment, she felt she would not care if she never saw it again.

'No,' she whispered.

'Good. Then as soon as your father

can spare you, I suggest you come up to the hall. I shall employ you as — let me see, a maid.'

'Yes, Lady Raglan,' Eli murmured, swallowing her disappointment.

Somehow, she had expected something a little less, well, ordinary. She looked up to find Lady Sara watching her, a mischievous grin playing over her features.

'But as for your real duties,' she remarked, 'well, Miss Owen, you shall just have to wait and see.'

'Yes, Lady Raglan.'

'Aunt Sara.'

Neither of them had noticed Richard making his way towards them, a concerned look on his face.

'Is everything all right, Aunt Sara?'

'Of course, my dear,' she replied, lacing up her boot once more. 'The young lady was most helpful.'

Boot secured, she took his hand as he helped her up from her resting place.

'And now a cup of tea, I think.'

'You must be frozen, Aunt. It's warm

in there, such an amazing place to find right on the top of a mountain.'

As they set off towards the hut, Lady Raglan turned back briefly to Eli, speaking in Welsh once more.

'And your duties, young woman, you will find do not include falling in love with this rather charming young nephew of mine.'

Eli felt herself growing a deep beetroot shade. She found Richard, who thankfully had not understood a word of the conversation in Welsh, eyeing her confusion with mild curiosity, and pulled herself together.

'Of course, Lady Raglan,' she murmured.

4

The small cart rattled its way from the small village of Llanberis, on its weekly mission of taking supplies up the steep and winding road to the small guest-house at Pen-y-Pass. This was the favoured starting point for those unwilling to make the long trek to Snowdon's summit from sea level. The cart came to a halt outside a large, iron gate almost overcome by the surrounding ivy.

'Eli, are you sure about this?'

The driver, a sturdy, weather-beaten man, past the first flush of youth, but with every appearance of being strong and active, eyed the gate in deep suspicion, rather as if he wished for a brace of pistols to be hidden in the backpack secured next to his feet.

'Mrs Hughes would certainly have had you back, had you asked, and the

Raglans, well, they have a certain reputation, you know.'

'So I've heard,' Eli said, smiling. 'Though I don't expect Lady Sara has a mad wife to keep in the attic, Tam, whatever else the village might say.'

Tam Cadwaladr grinned, and scratched the greying curls of his thick dark hair.

'I should hope not, though you never know what the old man might have left for her. Always afraid Queen Victoria was about to invade Wales and throw him out of the place to make way for one of her courtiers, was old man Raglan. They say he kept oil ready for the boiling in the attics, and cannon all primed on the roof, ready to make his last stand.'

'Really?'

Any last doubts Eli might have had about her decision flew off somewhere into the cloud swirling around the steep side of the ridge rising above them.

'Oh, and more, they say. Taught Lady Sara to shoot almost as soon as she could stand, and brought a fencing master all the way from Paris.'

'So she could fight the English, too, you mean?' Eli exclaimed.

A vision of Lady Sara, wielding a sword with one hand, and letting down whole bucketfuls of boiling oil with the other, flashed into her mind. She swallowed a giggle.

'That was the old man's idea, not Lady Sara's as it turned out. Not at all, in fact. She was always a wild one. Off up Snowdon, hiring me or your dad as a guide, as often as she could. And when she couldn't, off up to all sorts of things I'm quite sure your dad would not be wanting me to tell you about. And then of course there was the fencing master. Even old mad-dog Raglan should have known better than to trust her with that fencing master. The Raglans never lived that one down, I can tell you.'

Eli could have stayed and listened for the rest of the day. Tam had worked as a guide on Snowdon for as long as Dad had run the refreshment hut on the summit, and Eli never tired of his stories. Tam was a proper guide, one who knew the mountain like a friend, not like the many charlatans who, seeing a profit to be made, called themselves guides but often couldn't even find the correct path, and led their poor victims into all kind of trouble.

Tam Cadwaladr was the kind of guide who could find every secret place of every flower and fern sought out by collectors. He even, it was rumoured, knew the best sites for the very rare, and much sought-after Snowdon Lily, and kept them a closely guarded secret from the sorts of collectors who would dig up the entire species to add to their fame, even if it meant there were no plants left on the mountain.

But down in the village, the church clock struck the half hour, with a timely reminder that unless she hurried she would be late. With a regretful sigh, Eli jumped out of the cart, lifted down her small bag, and made her way to the gate.

'Thank you for the lift, Tam,' she called, and smiled. 'And for the warning. I promise I'll keep my eyes sharp, and make sure to be very careful.'

'Well, she may have been wild,' Tam said thoughtfully, 'but I'll say this for her. Lady Sara never showed anything of old mad-dog's, er, peculiarities, shall we say. Always seemed quite sane enough to me.'

He gathered his reins and clicked his tongue at the patient pony, setting the cart in motion again.

'But any sign of nonsense, Eli, my dear, and you make your way straight home again. The Raglans are rich enough to be as mad as they like, but not to drag respectable young women, who could be hurt, into their little games.'

'Yes, Tam,' Eli murmured.

There was no sign of anyone in the little house at one side of the gate, so she lifted the latch and let herself in. She had to admit to just a few nerves as the gate clanged to behind her, shutting her out of sight of Tam, now making his way towards today's clutch of visitors breakfasting at his brother's hotel, in readiness for the climb ahead.

She suddenly felt alone, and more than a little trapped. A high, stone wall, almost completely swathed in overgrown ivy, surrounded her as far as she could see. Mature beeches lined each side of the driveway in front of her, setting the gravel in deep shadow, and leading into all kinds of undergrowth on either side. Out on the road in the sunshine, with Llanberis stretched out below, along the sparkling waters of the lake, and Tam's reassuring presence beside her, every tale of the Raglans' eccentricities she had ever heard down the years had seemed wildly exciting, amusing, even.

Now, in the dark tunnel between the walls, with just a distant glimpse of stone wall, and the hard glint of windows, she was not so sure.

'Well, too late now,' she told herself firmly.

She squared her shoulders, grasped her bag, and set off, feet crunching on the gravel with every step.

★ ★ ★

'Elinor Owen, is it?'

'Yes, Mrs Williams.'

'References?'

'Ma'am?'

Elinor blinked at the sparse, middle-aged woman in front of her.

'Your references, girl,' the housekeeper repeated impatiently. 'Have you brought them with you?'

'Yes, Mrs Williams.'

Eli brought out the letters from Mrs Hughes and the teachers at the Sunday School, and placed them into the waiting hands.

'Mmm.' Mrs Williams sniffed, clearly unimpressed. 'No experience, I see.'

Eli felt it was better not to answer this. Oh, why on earth had she thought that Lady Sara herself would be there to greet her and tell her what her duties

52

were expected to be, instead of being hustled down into the bowels of the servants' quarters?

Maybe it had been all a mistake on her part. Maybe Lady Sara had never meant all those tantalising hints of special duties, or maybe she had changed her mind. Eli's immediate impulse was to run back to the safety of Llanberis as fast as her legs would take her and, from the look on the housekeeper's face, Mrs Williams would be only too glad to help her.

'Too old,' she was saying abruptly.

'Ma'am?'

'You're too old, girl, too old by half. I was fourteen when I took up my first position. Girls are still malleable at fourteen. Grown into habits of laziness and going their own way, afterwards. And you can read, I see.' She gave an even louder sniff. 'Most unsuitable, girls that can read. Gives them ideas. And I shall inform the mistress so, myself.'

'Yes, Mrs Williams,' Eli murmured,

keeping her eyes on the floor.

'I cannot imagine what Lady Sara was thinking of. Lord Raglan would never have put up with such nonsense.'

She glared at Eli, as if defying her to bring up any of those old rumours amongst the common people of the villages that there was any doubt whatsoever concerning the sanity of her former employer. Eli did her best to look demure, as if she had never heard a mention of boiling oil in her life. With one final sniff, Mrs Williams folded up the reference.

'Well, then, follow me,' she said.

Raglan Hall, Eli soon decided, was even more confusing inside than it was out. Outside, it had been a jumble of different stones and styles. There was even a round tower at one side which looked like the remains of some long-vanished castle. Inside, it was a maze of corridors and stairs, with rooms going off in all directions that soon had her utterly bewildered as to which way she was facing at all.

She caught a glimpse of the main stairway, deep in plush crimson carpet, and wood-panelled walls. Not that she was ever likely to even set foot on the lowest stair. Her route was the twisting, narrow servants' stairs, complete with bare, wooden treads and unpainted, stone walls that felt cold, even in the heat of the approaching summer. It must be truly freezing in winter, she noted with some dismay, almost as bad as the howling wind on Snowdon itself.

Mrs Williams led her to a tiny room at the very top of the house that she was to share with Miriam, a small, fair-haired girl, who looked about twelve in Eli's eyes, although she soon turned out to be just sixteen. Miriam, it seemed, was to teach her everything about her new duties.

'She's a Tartar, all right,' Miriam whispered, as Mrs Williams' dignified step could be heard retreating down into the house once more. 'Just keep your thoughts to yourself, and follow me, and you'll do fine. You'll soon pick it up, easy as can be.'

It might be easy as could be, but Eli was quite sure she would never pick up every detail of being a housemaid. She was strong and healthy, but in the weeks that followed, she found herself more tired than she had ever been. There were times when she was quite sure she would have fallen asleep on her feet, if she had ever stopped long enough to close her eyes.

She was up before dawn, emptying grates, cleaning them and blackening them before laying the fire for the day. The air was still cool, so fires were still needed in most of the rooms. After that, it was cleaning, and dusting, scrubbing floors and wiping windows, always taking care to stay out of the family's way, as if to keep an illusion that all the work that nearly broke her back each day was done by magic.

Occasionally, as she risked a quick glance out of a window she was wiping, at the sunshine playing on the shrubs and the lawns outside, she would catch a glimpse of Richard and his sister, strolling amongst the gardens, or setting out in the carriage on some expedition or other.

Lady Sara's niece and nephew were staying the entire summer, according to the information round the servants' table as they ate their evening meal. A good thing, too, for her ladyship, not to be alone in the big house. Young company would do her the world of good. Pity her sister couldn't have been there, too. A pretty, gentle kind of soul had been the younger Raglan sister. Such a tragedy dying so young, so soon after her husband, and leaving Mr Mayhew and Miss Catherine alone in the world. And so good of Mr Richard to leave his business interests and help his aunt in putting the old hall to rights.

'Those last years with the old man,' Mrs Jones, the cook, whispered one evening shaking her head, and clucking disapprovingly. 'The things that went on. It shouldn't have been allowed.'

'Looking for priest holes, he was,' Mr

Iago, the butler, added with the air of enjoying the scandal. 'Heaven knows why. And spent hours in the chapel, attempting to lift the stones.'

'Chapel?' Eli said, curiosity overcoming her.

She found them all staring at her as if they had forgotten her existence, or at least been quite convinced she didn't have a voice.

'In the grounds,' Mrs Jones said, with a motherly smile in her direction. 'Ruin, it is. Hasn't been used by the family for generations, but Lord Raglan was quite convinced there was something there. Heaven knows what, poor old gentleman. Saw enemies all around him, that he did.'

There was a general sighing and shaking of heads at this, and Eli didn't dare ask anything more.

An uneasy thought had stirred in her mind. Maybe Lady Raglan had inherited more of her father's eccentricities than anyone had yet realised. Maybe all that talk of being in need of someone she could trust, someone who could hide their thoughts from anyone who might be watching, maybe that was nothing more than her father searching for secret hiding places, and heaven knows what else. Maybe Lady Raglan had forgotten her existence entirely.

Eli swallowed hard. Well, if that was the case, she had no intention of being trapped here as the lowliest of lowly housemaids for ever. But how on earth could she possibly find her way out of here? It would scarcely have escaped the attention of anyone in Llanberis that she had taken up a post at Raglan Hall. If she left now, with no reasons, and with no references, why then, she might never find work again.

Just for a moment, she even regretted saying no to Griff Griffiths and his comfortable house on the Penrhyn estate, but then she pulled herself together, and came to her senses again. She would find a way out, somehow. And, as far as she was concerned, she didn't care if she never saw Sara

Raglan, or that disturbingly attractive nephew of hers, ever again. Besides, if Lady Sara turned out to be just as crazy as her father had been, heaven knows what secrets her nephew might have, lurking inside his brain.

And that, Eli decided, there and then, was something she was definitely not staying around to find out.

5

The next day, Eli woke just as the first light before dawn crept its way through the attic windows. She ached from head to toe, while her mind was still racing with the wild dreams that had whirled their way around in her head all night. In the little bed at the other side of the room, Miriam was still sound asleep.

For a while, Eli shut her eyes and lay as still as she could, but it was no good. Sleep just would not come. Quickly and quietly, so not to disturb the all-too-brief rest of her friend, Eli slipped into her clothes, and slipped down through the quiet house, and out through a small door at the back of the kitchen.

The air outside was cool, with almost a touch of frost hanging in the stillness. Under her feet lay thick dew in a white network of cobwebs on the lawn and over the shrubs. For a few minutes she walked not caring where she went, just glad to be out in the fresh air after so long. The sun began to rise, sending the cobwebs shimmering with water droplets, and colour appearing in the leaves of the trees.

She should turn back before anyone else began to stir and might notice her escape. Just as she turned, an arch of stone peeping through the beech leaves caught her eye. It was a pale stone, with just a hint of terracotta in its weatherbeaten glow between the green. Between the arch there lay a delicate, carved network of stone, which looked as if it had once been the foundation for a stained glass window.

Of course! The chapel Mrs Jones had been telling her about only yesterday. Eli hesitated, but a quick glance back at the house showed no sign of movement yet. She just couldn't resist and pushed her way through the trees.

There was no mistaking — it was the chapel all right. There was no roof, and apart from the arch of the window, the sides were all broken and crumbling, and almost completely obscured in ivy. So this was where Lady Sara's father had come, searching for something within these rotting walls! With a slight shiver, Eli stepped a little closer. The wall nearest her had almost fallen away, leaving a view of the inside of the chapel.

A cold shiver went down Eli's spine. If that was the case, heaven knows what Lady Sara might be wanting her to do! References or no references, she shouldn't remain here for a moment longer. In fact, she wouldn't even go back to the house at all, just go down the driveway and out on to the Llanberis road, and walk all day if she had to. With a sudden sense of urgency, she turned back towards the door.

'Ouch!'

The voice came from beneath her feet. Eli nearly jumped out of her skin.

'I'm sorry,' she faltered, eyes seeking out the source, half expecting a vampire at least to appear from beneath the stone lid.

'That was my foot, you know,' the voice came once more.

There was movement next to the stone casket as something that was definitely a leg was moved swiftly out of her way. Well, there was no ghost that Eli had ever heard of that wore muddy trousers tucked into worn, and even muddier boots. Taking a deep breath, she followed the direction of the foot and peered round the corner of the casket. No, decidedly not a ghost.

The man propped up against the adjoining ivy-strewn wall, with his head resting on a tattered backpack, was pale, but pulling his coat together to keep out the cold, and watching her with a pair of deep blue eyes that had nothing ghostly about them at all. He pulled himself up a little, as if in an attempt to rise to his feet, and winced.

'You will have to forgive my manners, though. This damned ankle of mine . . .'

'Are you all right?' Eli demanded.

'The better for seeing you,' he replied, with a wide, and undeniably charming smile.

'That wasn't what I asked,' Eli said, frowning at him and ready to take to her heels towards the safety of the house at any moment.

A ghost, maybe not, but a spy, thief or murderer, or all three together! The stranger was young, and decidedly good-looking beneath that tousled mop of fair hair, and his clothes, while in need of cleaning and a little mending in places, were of the best material and tailoring money could buy. He had the look of the well-to-do students and businessmen Eli had often seen on the mountains, who spent their vacations climbing Snowdon, and searching for ever rarer and more exotic ferns to add to their conservatories back in the leafy suburbs of London or Birmingham, in order to spend the winter impressing their neighbours with their daring.

The trouble was, he didn't look in the least distressed, as might be expected from a climber lost in the dark on the mountain looming up above them, knowing that his friends must be searching frantically through the night, putting their own lives at risk, while fearing the worst. All in all, a thief seemed the most likely prospect. She should run, call for help, and ensure the local constabulary arrived as quickly as possible. On the other hand, that smile of his was really very charming.

'And don't tell me I did the damage, either,' she added, severely.

'I'd much rather it had been you,' he returned. 'Then I could have blackmailed you into being my nurse and the pain would have been more than worth it.'

'Yes, I'm sure,' Eli replied, unimpressed by this gallantry. 'But I think you'd be better employing your time making your way back to the road to Llanberis. The family will be up in a few hours, and they won't take kindly to strangers sleeping in their chapel, if you ask me.'

'This stranger had no intention of sleeping in their chapel,' the injured man replied. 'And has no intention of staying here all day, either. Give me your hand.'

'You want me to pull you up?' she said, eyeing him with suspicion.

'That's the idea. Doesn't offend your modesty, I hope.'

'Of course not.'

'And you are not given to fainting after any exertion, I take it.'

'Hardly. Ladies first.'

'Then you are not a lady?' he responded, with a mischievous gleam in his eye.

It was a very disarming kind of mischief and all of a sudden, Eli found herself smiling.

'Certainly not. So if you are a fortune hunter with an eye to compromising my reputation so I am forced to marry you, think again. I have nothing to do with the Raglan household, except be the lowliest maid.'

'So this is indeed Raglan Hall,' he remarked, thoughtfully.

'Yes.'

Suddenly, the laughter went out of

her. Lady Raglan's father might have become insane, but Jacques, up on Snowdon, with his vague threats, had been real enough. Jacques had seemed to think the Eagle Stone was real, and Lady Sara had accused him of searching the house for it. Maybe this rather-too-charming stranger was more than just a common thief.

'Good,' the stranger was saying, taking her hand with a strong clasp. 'Then you can help me up.'

Well, she could hardly leave him there. Eli braced herself, and pulled. As she did so, he gave an instant yelp of pain, and fell back against the stone once more.

'Damn!' she heard him mutter. 'Of all the . . . '

'Let me see.'

For an experienced mountain walker like Eli, it took only a moment to establish that he was at least not feigning his agony. The ankle was badly swollen. He had partially unlaced his boot, but the sides where still pressing on the injury.

'Can you move it at all?'

'Do you want me to howl like a dog?' he returned.

'No, of course not. I'm trying to see if it's broken or not.'

'Sorry.'

His glance was apologetic. He moved the foot experimentally, drawing in his breath sharply as he did so. But at least it moved.

'It doesn't seem to be a break, not a bad one at least.'

As gently as she could, Eli unlaced the rest of the boot and removed it.

'That should feel a little easier. I'll go and fetch help from the house.'

'No!'

His voice was sharp. Eli frowned at him, suspicions flooding back.

'Well, I can't just leave you here, and you're not going to get far with that ankle,' she retorted. 'What else do you propose I do? The gardeners will begin work in a few hours, and you'll be found anyway.'

'No need to disturb the entire house.

Tell Richard . . . '

'Mr Mayhew?'

Eli blinked. The plot thickened. If this was all a plot of Jacques, surely Richard hadn't even seen him until that day on Snowdon, or so it seemed. Perhaps that had all been a lie, after all. As far as she could tell, Lady Sara had scarcely known her nephew and niece until her recent return to her homeland. Who knows what their real motive might be in accompanying her into the distant wilds of Wales for the summer?

'Yes. Richard Mayhew. He is staying here, isn't he?'

'Yes.'

'Good. Fetch him. No-one else, do you hear? Tell him it's Peter, from when he was up at Oxford.'

He fished out a thin gold chain from around his neck, slipped it over his head, and placed it into Eli's hand.

'Take this. He'll know who you mean.'

Eli hesitated, gazing down at the chain coiled in her palm. At the centre lay a gold ring, small, and very plain, with some kind of writing etched into its centre. She looked down at him. The blue eyes were on hers, pleading with her. They were mesmerising, those eyes, deep and earnest, and with the kind of look that could make a slave from a heart far harder than Eli's.

'I'll do my best,' she murmured and with the ring tightly hidden in her hand, she made her way quickly back to the house.

★   ★   ★

'Mr Mayhew.'

Eli tapped as loud as she dared once more on Richard's door. She gave a quick glance around. The corridor was deserted. It was still only just past dawn, and only the most lowly of the servants were beginning to stir. All the same, she dreaded anyone hearing her and coming to investigate.

Trying to make her way into a gentleman's bedroom at this hour of the morning! If she was caught, it would be instant dismissal, and all kinds of rumours flying round the village for years to come, and her reputation would never be the same again, and how Griff Griffiths would triumph over that. No doubt he would take the greatest of pleasure in telling anyone who would listen that he had soon seen through her industrious and innocent exterior, and found she was nothing more than a common slut no decent man should associate with, let alone marry.

Eli gritted her teeth, and tried again.

'Mr Mayhew.'

This time the door was opened, and Richard Mayhew, with his dark hair wild, and a dressing-gown pulled hastily around him, was blinking at her in astonishment, and some alarm.

'Is it my sister?' he demanded.

'No.' Eli shook her head vigorously. 'Or Lady Sara,' she added quickly.

'Well?'

Eli found herself going slowly scarlet.

His feet were bare, and the dressing-gown was rather more open than he might have intended, revealing a well-toned chest beneath the opening of his nightshirt. Heat was creeping through Eli, all the way from the bottom of her toes to the top of her head, sending a rather pleasant tingling sensation through her veins, and sending her mission straight out of her head for the moment.

'Well?'

His obvious irritation brought her back to her senses.

'Your friend,' she muttered.

He was frowning at her, clearly with a strengthening opinion that she had lost her mind. His hand tightened on the door handle, as if to shut it once more.

'Your friend, Peter,' she shot out. 'He's hurt. He needs your help.'

She held out the ring. He stared down at the small object for a moment, then she found herself being pulled unceremoniously inside his bedroom, and the door shut firmly behind her.

'Where did you get this?' Richard demanded.

He was so close she could smell his soap, and the faint lingering of cigars from last evening's dinner with several of the local families. In the dip in his collarbone, she could make out the pulse, and the rapid beating of his heart. It was all quite deliciously distracting.

'You can talk, can't you?'

His exasperation stung her back to the present.

'I told you,' she replied. 'Your friend, Peter. He said he was up at Oxford with you. He's in the chapel.'

'And what on earth is he doing there?'

'How on earth should I know?' she retorted indignantly. 'I just came across him. He's hurt.'

'Hurt? How badly?'

'Just his ankle. He must have twisted it. It doesn't appear to be broken. I checked,' she added, tartly, as he began frowning at her again. 'He asked me to come and fetch you, he didn't want anyone else to know, for some reason. I can inform Lady Raglan, if you prefer.'

'That won't be necessary.' He was eyeing her closely. 'I've seen you before, haven't I?'

'I'm a maid. I work here,' she snapped, before she could stop herself.

'I didn't mean that,' he replied then he smiled. 'I'm not that unobservant, you know, whatever else you might think of your employers.'

Eli lowered her eyes. She was now inside his room. If he wanted to get rid of her, and probably hounded out of Llanberis to boot, all he needed to do was to make sure someone found her there. Her thoughts were answered by a quiet laugh.

'Don't worry,' he remarked. 'I'm no supporter of slavery, or servitude, and it will come to me, soon enough.' He was serious again. 'And meanwhile, I need your help. Whatever trouble Peter is in, I'd rather keep it from my aunt for the moment. I'm sure I can trust your discretion.'

Eli bit her lip. She was supposed to be Lady Raglan's eyes and ears, but then Lady Raglan had never even spoken to her from the moment she arrived. Slowly, she nodded her head.

'Good girl. Now, could you escape back to the chapel before we cause the scandal of the year?'

He caught her hot blush, and a smile reached his eyes and lingered there.

'I'll join you as soon as I've made myself a little more respectable.'

Eli had never escaped a room so fast. There was still no-one to be seen, and she fled out into the coolness of the dawn air.

6

The injured man was just as Eli had left him. He looked up anxiously as she reappeared.

'Did you speak to Richard?'

'Yes. He's following in a moment.'

'Thank heaven!'

'I've brought you this.'

She placed the blanket she had removed from the laundry on her way out over him as best she could.

'Thanks.' He was shivering slightly. 'Don't know about the beauties of the dawn, but it's damned cold, I can tell you,' he remarked, with an apologetic grin.

Eli smiled.

'When climbers are injured on the mountains it's always the cold once they stop moving that is the greatest danger,' she said. 'You'll be fine once we get you inside.'

'Stupid thing to do,' he muttered, ruefully. 'Of all the stupid things to do, trip over in the dark. Not exactly heroic, eh? I bet you'd have found me much more interesting if I'd had a sword run me through, or a bullet lodged in my guts.'

'No, thank you,' Eli replied. 'At least with a twisted ankle you are quite likely to live a few years longer.'

'Little recompense for the indignity.'

She found he was eyeing her closely.

'Does my rescuer have a name?'

'Elinor. Elinor Owen.'

'Elinor. Pretty name. A queen's name.'

'Not this Elinor,' she returned.

'Maybe not.'

The blue eyes could be uncomfortably penetrating, she discovered, as if their owner was inspecting her through and through.

'But not exactly an illiterate housemaid, either. In fact, Elinor Owen, you are quite a puzzle, all in all. Worthy of one of Lady Raglan's puzzles, I should have guessed.'

'I don't know what you mean.'

'No? You mean in your housemaid duties, if that is indeed the guise you go under, it hasn't escaped your notice that no-one close to the good lady is ever quite what they seem?'

Eli blinked. His eyes narrowed at her silence, in something that approached concern.

'Because if I am mistaken, Miss Owen, I should warn you to find your way out of here as soon as you can. Trouble has a habit of following Lady Sara wherever she goes, and it is always the kind of trouble that can lead the unwary into serious harm.'

There was a moment's silence.

'I can take care of myself,' she replied at last, fighting down an unpleasant, quivery feeling, deep in her stomach.

'Oh, I've no doubt of that, in ordinary circumstances, but then Lady Sara has never specialised in ordinary circumstances.'

Before Eli could rely, a colony of rooks, resting in the trees a little distance away, took to the air, their raucous cries filling the dawn silence. She found a hand placed in a warning manner on her arm.

'That must be Richard,' she murmured, cold, despite herself, creeping up her spine.

He shook his head.

'Wrong direction,' he returned in a whisper, and began to pull himself painfully farther back behind the cover of the stone casket. 'There was someone in the forest a few hours ago. I was so certain they had gone. You'd better make yourself scarce. Get back to the house before you are seen. There will be no danger there.'

There was no mistaking his urgency, nor the crack of twigs in the distance, as if a stealthy tread were making its way towards them.

'It's me they're after, not you. Go on!'

Eli shook her head.

'I'm not leaving you,' she muttered, stubbornly.

Whoever Peter was, and whatever he might have been planning, arriving in the dark, she couldn't leave him here helpless, even if it was only the local constabulary coming to arrest him. It would be like leaving a wounded animal alone to its fate. Quickly, trying to hurt him as little as possible, she helped him drag himself farther back into the cover of long grass behind the large stone casket.

The next snap of a twig was close. Before she could move, Peter had pulled her down so that she was curled up next to him, with her head on his chest, and the rapid thunder of his heart filling her ears. Instinctively, Eli shut her eyes, and held on tight. She felt his arms close around her.

It seemed like an age that they lay there, breathing as lightly as possible. A crash of stones close to had Eli opening her eyes again. Someone was making their way between the grave-stones and monuments, and seemed to have dislodged the cover of one of the caskets. The stone was pushed again, as if the intruder was determined to look inside. Eli found her own heart beginning to race to match Peter's.

If the newcomer were prepared to move a heavy slab in their search, then the grasses and shadow of their corner would certainly not protect them. Slowly, stealthily, one hand reached out and felt for the nearest stone. If there was one thing certain, she was not about to give up without a fight.

'Damn it all, man!'

She could have wept with relief. There was no mistaking the voice. It was Richard Mayhew, loud and indignant.

'Have you no respect for the dead? If it's gold you're after, I can assure you there is nothing here.'

'My dear sir . . . '

A shiver went through Eli. She knew those smooth tones, not in the least perturbed by being caught vandalising a family chapel any more than he had been by the sudden appearance of Lady

Raglan outside Dad's refreshment hut on the top of Snowdon.

'A thousand apologies. No disrespect intended. As so close a friend of your venerable aunt, I was merely satisfying my interest in the so-famous Raglan ancestry. Such a sad ruin, sir. I believed Lady Sara has expressed an interest in restoring the Raglan chapel.'

'My aunt has done nothing of the sort.'

Eli grinned. Richard Mayhew could certainly sound the pompous and unreasonable landowner when he chose to. She expected the sound of a shotgun being primed at any moment!

'And you will oblige me, sir, by removing yourself as quickly as possible. Lady Sara expressed herself quite clearly at our previous meeting. She considers herself no friend of yours, and, as such, you are not welcome here. Now leave. If I hear of you within the estate again I shall not hesitate in having you arrested for trespass.'

There was a moment's pause.

'Interesting thing, the past.' Jacques appeared not to have heard him. 'So many unexpected little things waiting there, just ready to be found. Take all these gravestones, all with a story to tell. And not all you might want the local villagers to hear. Take your aunt's past.'

'Blackmail?' Richard's voice was harsh.

'My dear sir, I would never do anything to damage dear Sara's health, or reputation. Our friendship goes back too far, and is much too deep, for me to even think of such a thing.' He gave a low chuckle. 'Although, being so young, and, shall we say, so respectable a relative, I doubt Sara would have told you just how — '

'Get out!'

Richard was no longer playing a part. He was furious.

'And don't let me ever find you here again.'

'Tsk, tsk, Mr Mayhew.' Jacques was openly amused. 'The English overblown sense of the proprieties. Little wonder Sara took the first fencing master she could find, and made her way to, shall we say, more open climes? Give the dear lady my kind regards, and I trust we shall be renewing our acquaintance before long.'

The next moment, he could be heard making his way into the distance, whistling casually as he went.

Richard muttered, irritably. He was silent for a few minutes, clearly waiting until the unwelcome intruder was safely out of earshot.

'Peter?' he hissed at last.

'We're here.'

Eli hastily attempted to free herself from Peter, who seemed quite unwilling to let her go so that she was still half entwined as Richard strode over to their hiding place.

'We couldn't go any farther,' she murmured, aware of her face flushing scarlet at his frown, and struggling to her feet. 'If you hadn't arrived so fast, he'd have found us, for certain.'

'Good-looking species of guardian angel you have here,' Peter remarked, with a grin. 'You should have told me, Richard. I'd have arrived here sooner, had I known.'

'I'm certain,' Richard replied acidly, then turned to Eli. 'Are you all right?'

She nodded.

'I'm sorry, Richard, this is all my fault. Ireland was not as safe as I had thought. Jacques and his men found us all right. I was the only one who managed to make a clean getaway. I knew Lady Sara had returned to Raglan Hall, so I took the first boat I could find. It seemed safer to come through the mountains, so I jumped ship just down the coast, and came over the pass late last night. The road seemed clear enough so I made my way down.'

He gave a quick glance in Eli's direction.

'I was hoping to surprise you at breakfast. Then this happened. I got this far and lost sight of the house in the trees. And once I'd stopped I just couldn't seem to get back on my feet again. I'm afraid I seem destined to cause your family trouble.'

'Not at all. I'm just glad you could make it this far.'

'The ankle's twisted, but it doesn't seem to be broken,' Eli put in.

She found Richard frowning at her again.

'Oh, I'd trust her word, if I was you,' Peter added. 'A regular mountaineer is Miss Elinor.'

'That was it! I knew it would come to me. You're the young woman from the refreshment hut on Snowdon. You assisted my aunt with her boot.'

'Yes,' Eli said, a little defiantly.

'I thought she was up to something, speaking to you only in Welsh like that, especially now I discover there is nothing limited about your English. I take it you recognised who it was hunting you and Peter just now?'

Eli nodded.

'And has my aunt told you anything more?'

'No.'

'Well, she was obviously intending to.'

'I haven't even seen her since I arrived,' Eli protested.

'That's Aunt Sara. Never trust anyone completely until you are sure. Did you have any instructions?'

'No, not that I understood. She just said I could hide what I thought, and pretend I didn't follow what was said in English, and that she might have need of it at some time.'

Lady Sara's final instruction shot back into her mind, but she wasn't about to tell him of that one.

'Did she now,' Richard said, watching her thoughtfully.

'I thought she must have changed her mind.'

'Oh, if she had done that, you'd have known about it, and no mistake. And I'm afraid you are in this, willing or not, Miss Owen. Now, our problem is to get Peter here into the house without being seen.'

Eli blinked.

'I'm afraid our friend, Jacques, there, is under the impression Peter will know the whereabouts of the Eagle Stone. I have no doubt Jacques has his people watching the house, maybe even watching from within the house, and if he has any suspicion Peter has arrived here, he'll leave no stone, if you'll pardon the expression, unturned to find him.'

'But we can't wait until it is dark again,' Eli protested. 'Jacques could come back at any moment, and besides . . . '

She glanced over to Peter, who, despite doing his best to appear cheerful, was even paler than before, while his frame was visibly racked with the onset of shivering. He was either chilled to the bone or running a fever, or possibly both, and to be out in the damp air much longer could lead to serious consequences for an injured man.

'You're right.'

Richard understood her look in an instant. A faint smile played around his lips.

'In which case, Miss Owen, I have no choice but to reveal to you one of the Raglan family's most closely-guarded secrets. I expect I should really cut your throat afterwards, to prevent you spreading it further. But since I'm not exactly fond of the sight of so much blood, I might allow you to survive.'

'Very gentlemanly, I'm sure.'

'Oh, not as much as my friend Peter, here,' he retorted dryly. 'He seemed determined to protect you to the last just now. He appeared to be holding you remarkably closely for a sick man.'

'I didn't ask him to,' she snapped back. 'I'm perfectly capable of looking after myself, thank you.'

Peter was clearly growing worse by the minute, and in no position to defend her. She scowled ferociously in her own defence. To her surprise, Richard chuckled.

'Peter is accustomed to women falling at his feet and obeying his every word,' he replied with a grin. 'I'm afraid he'd find you rather too hot to handle.'

'And you?' she demanded, the blood rushing to her head as her temper rose.

For a moment, he looked a little startled, but then the smile was back again.

'Oh, I like my women fiery. In fact, the fierier, the better.'

'I didn't mean — '

She stopped dead, confusion overcoming her. Of course, that was exactly what she had meant, but she had never had any intention of throwing herself at him. She collected her dignity together.

'Really? I am sure you have a plentiful collection of those in London. I've heard it is full of independently-minded ladies.'

'Not nearly so much as I would have liked,' he replied softly.

She couldn't quite suppress the rising of her colour at his tone, and was forced to turn back towards Peter to escape his gaze.

'So how are we going to get him out of here?' she demanded, feeling this was a safer subject, as well as a far more urgent one.

'By following close on the heels of Mad-dog Raglan, I suspect,' came the unexpected reply.

Suspecting him of beginning to tease her again, she brought out her scowl once more.

'Oh, don't worry. He wasn't nearly as crazy as the stories would have you think. The part about Queen Victoria and the invading army was true, but then the English have made a habit of invading Wales over the years, so really, you could hardly blame him.'

He grinned.

'He had me down as his heir for a while, until he decided an even better plot would be to force Sara home, for a while at least. Oh, not that I mind in the least, you understand. I could never have stepped into Sara's place like that. But old Raglan did have me hunting in here, when I was a child. Not for treasure you understand.'

He moved amongst the caskets, inspecting the inscriptions.

'What, then?'

'Aha, here it is. I knew I'd remember it.'

He kneeled down and began brushing the moss from the slab beneath his feet.

'Priest holes, of course. Secret passages, rather. I'm afraid to say the Raglans were never much ones for idealism. I doubt if any would have provided refuge for any kind of priest unless the price was high enough. But highway robbery, kidnap, smuggling, now that was a Raglan speciality. There are hidden passages all over the estate. Here we are.'

He lifted the stone. As he did so, a dark hole opened up beneath, with steps making their way down into the darkness below. He reached in, and brought out a small lamp, the end of a candle, and a small box containing a flint and some kindling.

'There you are, you see. The old man insisted that we left it all prepared. I never thought there would come a day I'd bless him for it.'

He turned back to Eli.

'Not afraid of the dark, are you?'

'No. Not really.'

'Good. I'm afraid I'm going to have to leave you in there, with the lamp, of course. The passage goes right under the house. I'll need to put the stone back and make it look as if no-one has been, in case Jacques comes nosing round here again, and meet you from the passage in the house. It won't take long. I'll be as fast as I can.'

He took her hand.

'I can't force you into this, Miss Owen. If you prefer, I can persuade my aunt to open the door into the house.'

'No! No, I'll be fine,' Eli said hastily.

'I knew you would.'

His free hand brushed her cheek, so gently and so swiftly she had no time to protest.

'And I will never let any harm come to you, Elinor. I swear it.'

And before she had time to catch her breath, he was turning back to help Peter towards the darkness of the steps.

7

The cold was creeping into her very bones. Eli shivered, and wrapped the blanket closer around the unconscious form of Peter beside her. The lamp flickered for a moment, as if caught in a strong breeze that threatened to blow it out.

'He'll be here soon,' she muttered. 'Just a few more minutes.'

Peter muttered, and stirred in his sleep. Eli placed her hand on his forehead. It was burning, and covered in small beads of sweat. She swallowed. For all his charm and his cheerfulness, it seemed Peter had been far worse than he had allowed her to believe. She cursed herself for never having thought to check for any further injuries than his twisted ankle. He hadn't shown any obvious signs, but he could well have cracked ribs from when he fell, and lying there in the cold dew after the exertions of walking through the mountains all day could easily lead to an infection on his lungs.

She looked down at the pale face in front of her in the uncertain light. There was a deep frown between his brows, and he was murmuring to himself. By the sound of it, he was trying to warn some phantom companions of an urgent danger in a language she had never heard before. Before, he had seemed simply an English gentleman, the kind who would have joined Richard for the rare privilege of a university education. And he still was, except for the lamplight throwing a shadow beneath the well-defined, high cheekbones that suddenly made him appear altogether alien.

He must be from Milat, of course! How many more were there ready to risk their lives to save their Eagle Stone, she wondered. And how many more, like Jacques, ready to kill to retrieve it?

Eli shivered again. Outside the small

circle of lamplight, a vast darkness seemed to open up around her. She could just make out the sides of the tunnel, hewn out of rock and oozing a steady stream of water that slithered down the slimy walls. Water dripped from the rock above her, splashing into the puddles on the floor. She could hear the drips echoing into the far distance, into the unknown length of the passageway.

The slab above her was sealed back into place once more. She had only a thumbnail's height of oil in the lamp, and a small end of candle. Once those were gone she would be alone in the darkness with a man who, if help did not come soon, would most surely die.

Peter muttered once more, louder this time, and more urgent. One arm fought itself free of his covering, lashing out as if to fight away some unseen assailant.

'It's all right,' Eli said quickly. 'It's all right, Peter, you're safe now. Richard will be here in a moment.'

Her voice seemed to calm him, and he settled once more. Gently, Eli took hold of the arm and placed it back on to his chest. His fingers, she could feel, were cold and lifeless. Richard had to come soon! She began to wrap the blanket back around him, to keep in as much warmth as she could. As she did so, she felt a warm stickiness ooze on to her fingers. Blood! It couldn't be.

There had been no sign of any injury to his chest as he had lain propped up against the chapel wall. His jacket was light coloured. She would surely have seen any blood creeping through. Hastily, Eli brought the lamp closer to the injured man. There was no mistake. A dark stain was spreading itself slowly across the pale material of his jacket.

'Peter!'

Eli gazed at him in despair. He seemed to be deeply unconscious, by now, and burning up even more than before.

How could such a wound have appeared so suddenly? Sickness churned in Eli's stomach. There were only two people who had been near the injured walker since she had first caught sight of him — herself and Richard, and she certainly hadn't inflicted a wound that could cause so much bleeding. In her ears came the distant echoing of footsteps, accompanied by the longed-for flicker of a lamp, but, far from relief, Eli searched around desperately for some hiding place. If Richard wanted to get rid of Peter, then he certainly would not be leaving witnesses to his crime. But there was no escape, and the next moment she found Richard arriving at her side.

'How is he?' he demanded, lifting the lamp to inspect them both.

'He's hurt,' Eli said, clenching her fists.

They might not be much, but she wasn't giving up Peter without a fight. She saw Richard bend over her companion, the lamplight revealing the dark stain, now spreading rapidly.

'Damn!' he muttered, sounding concerned enough, but not in the least surprised. 'We'd better move fast. He must have opened that wound up again.'

'Wound?' Eli demanded, suspiciously.

Wounded men, especially with wounds that could bleed as well as this one, were not in the habit of wandering leisurely through the mountains. Climbing took all the strength of a fully-fit man. An injured one stood no chance at all.

'He was badly hurt earlier,' Richard replied.

He caught Eli's gaze.

'Oh, so you think I gave him a quick stab to the heart in passing, did you?' he added, his mouth in a tight line. 'Thank you for that vote of confidence, Miss Owen.'

'I didn't!' she protested, not too indignantly.

He might still be bluffing, and just biding his time, she considered.

But she wasn't about to pick any kind of fight down here when there was no way out. To her relief, Richard seemed to forget her suspicions immediately. He crouched down at Peter's side, and passed a hand over the burning forehead.

'Jacques would be very pleased with his handiwork,' he remarked, bitterly. 'Those earlier attempts of his might yet have killed him.'

'No!' Eli gazed at him in distress. 'They can't have done!'

'Jacques did his best,' Richard muttered. 'They killed the rest of Peter's family. I doubt if they'll stop with him.'

'For the Eagle Stone?' Eli said, in disbelief.

'Not exactly.' Her companion was silent for a moment. 'This is not child's play, Eli,' he said at last. 'It never is with my aunt. My mother was always trying to dissuade her from these adventures of hers, to swallow her pride and ask old Mad-dog Raglan to fund those expeditions. He might well have done, too, once she was seen in the papers, undertaking all kinds of outrageous explorations. But she wouldn't, insisting on funding it all herself.'

'How?'

The answer, Eli, had suddenly realised, was blindingly obvious, and it made her very nervous indeed.

'By working for Her Majesty's government. The best operative in the field, so I'm told. Lady Sara Raglan is a known eccentric, likely to turn up anywhere. Who would notice that her appearance is often where there is trouble, or likely to be trouble, and where Queen Victoria might need the help of a little espionage?'

'So she is a spy.'

Eli looked down at the unconscious man before her with new eyes.

'You're right,' Richard said, following her gaze. 'Milat was Aunt Sara's latest assignment. There had been rumours for months that the king's younger brother had joined with a group of businessmen and adventurers to over-throw his brother and have himself crowned king.'

'With the Eagle Stone.'

'Exactly. Sara was too late to prevent the coup, but she did manage to spirit away the Eagle Stone.'

'And Peter.'

'And Peter. He really was up at Oxford with me, you know. His mother was a cousin of Queen Victoria, so he was always destined for an English education. Not that it has done him much good, poor soul, apart, I suppose, from those times we managed to give his bodyguards the slip in the vacations and make our own adventures climbing the mountains round here, so at least he could find his way here. Unfortunately, that also means that Raglan Hall was the most obvious place for Jacques and his men to search for both the Eagle Stone and Pettrich Mikhail, the fugitive crown prince of Milat.'

Eli swallowed.

'I'm not sure I want to be a spy,' she said, a little shakily, and her companion gave a wry grin.

'Me neither. I'd far rather stick with

the intrigues of exporting timber, given the choice, but it looks as if neither of us has any choice now, any more than poor Peter did from the moment he was born.'

He gave her hand a reassuring squeeze, then picked up his wounded friend, and began to make his way back as fast as he could, motioning Eli to go on ahead with Peter's backpack, and the lamp.

The tunnel seemed to go on for ever. The floor sloped downwards, growing colder, and dripping even more furiously the farther they went. Wide puddles appeared in the floor, soaking the rim of her skirt, and sloshing icy water inside her boots, where it squelched, slowly, with every step she took. At last steps appeared out of the gloom, carved into the rock.

They might be harder work than the downward-sloping floor, but at least they were moving upwards towards the surface. It was a door that stopped their progress, a small, heavy door that appeared carved out of rock. Eli paused, searching with the lamp for some means of opening it, as Richard, breathing hard with the effort of his heavy burden, caught up with her.

'A lever, to the side,' he muttered, hoarsely.

Eli scrabbled around for a little before she found the wooden handle. She pushed it down, hard, and the door swung open with an unwilling creak. The light spilling through nearly blinded her.

'Hush,' Richard whispered urgently. 'Be as quiet as you can. We are inside the house. Our voices could betray us.'

Eli nodded, and paused to extinguish the lamp, before closing the door once more. Then she followed Richard as silently as she knew how. They were behind the wooden panelling that lined most of the rooms of Raglan Hall, Eli discovered, as her eyes adjusted to the light. They were still in gloom, lit only by light filtering between the wood itself, and the occasional slit of a window cut into the stone walls on one side.

They were, she soon realised, in the very oldest part of the house. The tiny windows had the look of the openings in a castle, designed to allow arrows out, and no-one in. This part of Raglan Hall must have been a castle once! No wonder old Lord Raglan had invaders in his brain as his mind began to wander. He must surely have known of this network of passageways hidden behind the improvements to the hall, and realised that he was living where so many of his ancestors must have fought and died, protecting their lands from the invading English lords bent on improving their fortunes.

A network of passages it certainly was. Eli found doors that must open into several of the rooms, while other passages led away, some at one angle, some at another, some going down deep once more, some spiralling upwards as if towards some ancient battlements.

It was one of these flights of steps

that they followed, twisting up and up on stone, until they came to a kind of landing, with a door facing them. There, Richard laid Peter down gently on the floor at last, and stood for a moment, bent over and trying to catch his breath.

'If I'm ever tempted to take work hauling coal, or down a slate mine, remind me not to,' he remarked, with a rueful grin.

He leaned against the wall, wiping his face.

'And a strong man in a circus will never be an opening to me.'

He righted himself, and tapped smartly three times on the wooden panelling in front of him. There was a moment's pause, then the wood slid slowly back.

'Well?' a voice came from without.

'He's alive, but worse than I thought,' Richard replied.

'Well, it can't be helped. Bring him through, then.'

Richard picked up his burden once

more, and they stepped out of the secret passageway and into a richly-furnished bedroom. Blinded by the slant of morning sun streaming in through the windows, Eli stumbled a little. A firm hand reached out to steady her.

'There, young woman, I knew I was right about you. I said that I might be needing you, and that innocent-looking face of yours.'

Eli blinked hard, and found herself gazing into the sharp, watchful face of Lady Raglan.

'He'll live.'

Some time later, Sara Raglan finished washing the blood from her hands and wiped them dry.

'He must have opened up that wound again, but I can't see any sign of infection. The fever must be from being chilled for so long during the night. Given time and care he should recover well enough.'

'Thank goodness,' Richard breathed. 'When I saw all that blood, I thought we had lost him for certain.'

'Much longer, and we could have done,' Sara said grimly. 'If it hadn't been your quick thinking this morning, Eli, it could have been quite a different story.'

Eli blushed with pleasure.

'I'm glad I happened to find him,' she murmured, a little shyly.

If she had admired Lady Raglan before from the stories she had read about her fighting off savages and sailing down rapids, Eli now held her in more respect than ever.

There had, of course, been no question of fetching a doctor. It was Lady Raglan's skills that had dressed his wounds and made him as comfortable as she could in a small room adjoining her bedroom, which appeared to be her dressing-room, hidden from any casual observer entering her bedroom.

The three of them were now back in the largest of Lady Sara's rooms, which served as a private sitting-room.

'The question now,' Lady Raglan

said, thoughtfully, 'is how we are to proceed next.'

Whatever her considerations might have been, they were interrupted by a knock on the door.

'Come in!' Sara called, without a moment's hesitation.

'Excuse me, my lady.'

Eli instinctively stepped into the nearest shadow as Mrs Williams, the housekeeper, stepped inside, embarrassment and apologies on her thin face, along with just the faintest hint of triumph.

'I sorry to trouble you, ma'am.'

'Yes? What is it?'

'One of the new housemaids, ma'am. She appears to have gone missing. She was seen early this morning, walking out into the grounds, and she hasn't been seen since. She was said to be a respectable girl, ma'am, and we were informed she was reliable, and not at all the sort to just wander off like that.'

She couldn't quite keep the smugness from her voice.

'It seems, ma'am, that we were misinformed.'

'Elinor Owen, is it?' Lady Raglan said coolly.

'Why, yes, ma'am. You took her on in good faith, my lady, but you know how these people are. It might raise, well, high feelings against the estate if anything should be seen to have happened to her while under this roof.'

'Nonsense.' Sara was abrupt. 'Elinor is quite safe. She has been assisting me this morning. It's my maid, Hortense, who appears to have vanished without a trace.'

'Really, ma'am?'

The housekeeper sounded a little dubious, clearly thoughts of the reputed insanity of all the Raglan breed uppermost in her mind.

'Why, yes. It must have been Hortense you saw wandering off this morning, the shameless piece of baggage. Back to London to visit her young man, I shouldn't wonder. I warned her, if I saw sight or sound of him again I'd send her packing. Well, I'll not have her back. She's burned her boats, once and for all, I can tell you.'

'Yes, ma'am.' The housekeeper sounded understandably bewildered.

'So Elinor has been laying a fire for me, since no-one else came this morning.'

'My instructions were that you had no need of one today,' the housekeeper said, not quite managing to keep the irritation from her voice.

'Well, I changed my mind. That is a neat job you have done, Elinor. I'm pleased with you, very pleased indeed.'

The housekeeper's eyes widened as Eli took the hint and stepped out of the shadows. In the grate, a fire burned brightly, no doubt lit by Lady Sara herself, who seemed to have covered every eventuality with breathtaking thoroughness.

'In fact, since I appear to be without a maid for the foreseeable future, I think Elinor can fill the post quite nicely.'

'But, ma'am!'

The housekeeper's sense of decorum sent shock into her face. Housemaids didn't just suddenly become raised to the heights of a lady's personal maid in such an abrupt fashion! It was a long apprenticeship, and a long time working your way up through the ranks of the servants before any girl could even dream of such heady promotion.

'I'm not doing without a maid, and none of the other girls here seems to have a modicum of sense. At least Elinor here can follow instructions, after a fashion.'

Out of the corner of her eye, Eli discovered Richard Mayhew grinning to himself at this outrageous piece of play-acting from his aunt.

'Very well, ma'am.'

The housekeeper was defeated. Shaking her head as her only means of showing her disapproval of this highly-irregular state of affairs, she excused herself, and could soon be heard creaking down the stairs towards the kitchens below, no doubt to lash the rest of the servants with her tongue into working harder than ever to fill Eli's place, as well as their own.

For a moment, Eli felt sorry for Miriam, who could well bear the brunt of all this, but it couldn't be helped. She'd try and make it up to Miriam later. A thought struck her.

'Is that true, Lady Raglan?' she demanded. 'About your maid?'

This was too much of a coincidence! Surely Sara would never expect her just to accept it.

'Oh, Hortense is on the London train, all right. Well on her way, by now, I should hope, but, sadly for her, there is no young man in the case. I sent her myself, as soon as Richard told me of our visitor in the chapel. I had a little errand for her.'

'Are you sure about this, Aunt?' Richard was frowning. 'Jacques was watching the house carefully this morning.'

'And you think I didn't suspect that,

114

Richard?' Sara was chuckling to herself. 'The passageway to the chapel isn't the only one, you know, and Hortense has been with me long enough to be used to these kinds of emergencies. Don't worry, there will be no Hortense on the train. A nun, maybe, or even a young curate visiting his sick mother, while Hortense will have vanished entirely until her mission is accomplished.'

Lady Sara rubbed her hands, and appeared to be thoroughly enjoying herself.

'That fool, Jacques, should have known better than to attempt to take me on.'

This time she clapped her hands like a schoolma'am ordering her class.

'And now, to work! Richard, you must join your sister. I think for the moment, at least, it is better that you keep her in the dark. The less anyone knows about this business, the better.'

She rang the bell vigorously.

'And you and I, Eli, shall start with breakfast. I don't know about you, but such excitement always leaves me with an excellent appetite. And then we shall have to lay our plans.'

8

Eli paused in the summer sunshine, and stretched her aching back and arms with a yawn. She would have given anything to be able to lie down and go to sleep amongst the green grass of the Raglan gardens, but her precious moments of fresh air were very brief, and she was due back to the sickroom, secreted away inside the panelling of the house, almost immediately.

'Eli.'

She swung around to find Catherine Mayhew hurrying towards her, smiling a little shyly.

'Good morning, miss.'

'Is my aunt feeling better, Eli?'

'Yes, miss,' Eli said, blushing slightly.

Lady Sara's pretence of a slight fever to keep to her rooms for the past two days seemed to have done its work of keeping the household away, but Eli had no wish to tell a direct lie to anyone's face.

'It's just, everyone is so vague, and Richard won't tell me anything. Are you quite certain it is nothing serious?'

'Quite certain, miss,' Eli said, with a smile.

Lady Raglan was an active woman, unused to being cooped up for hours on end, and had been prowling round the rooms like a caged tiger since dawn. What with that, and her disgust at the delicate offerings of invalid food sent up by Mrs Jones with the very best of intentions, Eli was certain her employer would be unable to keep up this pretence for very much longer.

'Oh, I'm so pleased.'

Catherine smiled, more broadly this time, her pretty face lighting up with relief.

'It's such a beautiful day, it's a shame for anyone to have to keep to their beds.'

'Yes, miss,' Eli agreed.

'And don't tell her you saw me this morning, Eli.'

A touch of mischief entered the blue eyes, giving her more than a passing resemblance to her aunt.

'She's got this idea into her head that we shouldn't go anywhere in the grounds, but there can hardly be wolves or highwaymen at this time of day. And anyhow, doesn't everyone say the Raglans are always imagining some enemy or other sneaking towards them?'

Alarm stirred in Eli. Drat Lady Raglan for refusing to take Catherine into her confidence!

'I believe there have been prowlers seen in the grounds,' she said, sounding feeble in her own ears.

'Oh, but they would hardly venture here during the day,' Catherine said, smiling. 'And anyhow, I'm not going to go any farther than the flowerbeds. No-one who shouldn't be here would dare come out in full view of the house, and I'm not staying inside a moment longer.'

Eli sighed. Catherine might be only

half a Raglan, and scarcely looked like one at all, but she possessed the Raglan spirit all right.

'Yes, miss,' she murmured.

She had two choices — either to tag along behind Miss Mayhew, and dodge more awkward questions concerning Lady Sara's health, or she could find Richard to come out and deal with the problem. Catherine was already setting off with a swift and determined step across the lawn. No, it would take a Raglan to deal with a Raglan. Her brief enjoyment of fresh air forgotten, Eli raced inside the house.

She found Richard deep in conversation with Peter, who was by now sitting up in bed, pale, but with his fever almost gone.

'What is it, Eli?' he demanded at her breathless state.

'I'm sorry, Mr Mayhew, I didn't know what to do. Miss Catherine has taken herself off for a walk in the grounds.'

'Your elusive sister, eh, Richard?'

Peter remarked, who appeared to find this information amusing. 'The one you won't let me see nor sight nor sound of, eh?'

'Yes, and while you remain an incorrigible flirt it will stay that way,' Richard replied, dryly. 'You've enough young women falling at your feet without trying your luck with my sister, thank you very much.'

'Really? I thought I might make an ideal husband,' Peter returned. 'There have been plenty of fathers who have agreed with me these passed few years.'

Richard laughed.

'You will make an appalling husband, whichever unfortunate young lady is eventually pressed into marrying you,' he replied. 'Fathers have no idea of the realities of this kind of thing. Mainly, I suspect, their considerations lie with bloodlines and hard cash.'

'I do have some personal charms, you know,' Peter protested, a little hurt at this unflattering assessment.

'Of course, you do.' Richard smiled at

him. 'But you can't blame me for wanting to shield my sister from the — shall we say — rather fluid fortunes of your family?'

Peter gave a wry smile.

'I can see your point,' he admitted.

Eli listened to this exchange with curiosity. She discovered Richard frowning at her.

'Did Catherine say how far she was going?'

'Not far. Not into the trees. I did warn her about intruders, but she thinks they only come out at night, and I couldn't explain any further.'

Not that she knew anything to explain, she added to herself, ruefully. The entire business was a mystery to her.

'She should be safe enough.'

But Eli's unease had transferred itself to him. The next moment, Richard was on his feet and making for the door.

'Best to be certain,' he muttered. 'Wait here until I return.'

He closed the door of the little room,

and there was a moment's silence.

'You don't think she is in any real danger, do you?' Peter demanded at last.

'Probably not. Everyone's feeling a little jittery at the moment, that's all.'

'Because of me?'

'You couldn't help being injured, or your other troubles,' she muttered.

'But I could help coming here.' He sighed. 'Lady Sara was my last hope. Once they found my last hiding place I had nowhere else to go.'

He gave a wry smile.

'My father always told me to trust no-one but your Queen Victoria and Lady Raglan. And I was rather far from Windsor Castle, I'm afraid.'

'Where were you before?' Eli asked, curiously.

'Ireland. A small monastery in the south. Everyone thought I would be safe there.' He gave a wry smile. 'Trust that Frenchman never to give up.'

'Jacques, you mean?'

'What do you know of Jacques?' he

demanded, eyes narrowing.

'Nothing. He was up on Mount Snowdon when I first met Lady Sara. He seemed to have followed her all the way up there. He thought — '

She came to an abrupt halt.

'He thought?'

'He thought she was trying to hide the Eagle Stone up there, in King Arthur's cave.'

Her companion gave a grunt of laughter.

'Did he, indeed? Yes, that's just Lady Sara's style. Heaven knows how she managed to smuggle the stone out of Milat. Every road out of the place was guarded.' He tapped his injured side. 'They got me away over the mountains, after.'

He paused for a moment, his customary cheerfulness lost in dark memories. Then he shook them off once more with a determined air.

'But even then, not without a couple of border guards taking pot shots at us.' He sighed. 'I've always led a perfectly selfish life, I'm afraid. A close shave like that one, makes you think.'

He was silent for a moment.

'Still, Elinor, it was worth every moment of the journey that brought me to you.'

He took her hand in his, and kissed it, gently.

'I owe you my life, Eli, and I'll never forget that time in the tunnel, waiting in the darkness. Whenever I felt myself slipping away, there you were, holding my hand and urging me back towards life once more.'

His voice deepened.

'I'll never forget that, Eli, never. You have given me a new chance for life, and I intend to waste none of it. I don't want to spend my life with some empty-headed little miss, dreaming only of tiaras and her next ball gown. I need a woman of resourcefulness, and courage, at my side. I don't care what anybody says, or does. I have come to my senses at last.'

Gently, Eli tried to pull her hand

away, but his grip was very firm.

'So, what do you say, Elinor? My resourceful little mountaineer with the name of a queen, will you stand by my side and fight for justice, and freedom from tyrants?'

'Please, sir.' Eli blinked at him, uncertain whether to laugh or cry. 'You're still feverish, you don't know what you're saying. You hardly know me, and besides . . . '

'Oh, I know exactly what I'm saying,' he broke in, impulsively. 'It's not unknown, you know. My mother could have married a dozen or more kings and emperors, every one of them quite capable of swallowing up a hundred or more Milats, but instead, she married for love.'

'That's not quite the same,' Eli said.

'Who cares? I've played by their rules for long enough. I've considered every crown princess in Europe, and a few more besides, and not one of them could match up to the smallest finger on your right hand. And if Jacques gets hold of the Eagle Stone I shall be a private citizen for the rest of my life, dependent on the generosity of others. I have never been so sure of anything in my life before . . . '

His hand was pulled away abruptly, and Eli discovered Richard standing in the shadow of the door, watching them both with a scowl.

'Did you find your sister, my friend?' Peter asked.

'No.' The reply was short. 'Lady Raglan is organising a detailed search of the grounds.'

He gestured briefly towards Eli.

'And she's asking for you.'

'Of course. I'll come straight away,' Eli said quickly, escaping as fast as she could and following Richard down the stairs.

'That's a deep game you are playing, Miss Owen. I trust you know what you are letting yourself in for,' he said suddenly.

'I beg your pardon?'

Eli stopped dead on the landing of

the stairway, turning to face the fury in his voice with a temper rising to match his own.

'Have you any idea how his family, let alone his country, would react to your sudden — er — elevation, shall we say?'

'He hasn't got a country,' Eli snapped. 'I rather thought that was the point.'

'You know what I mean.'

'Unfortunately, I know exactly what you mean. The peasants should know their place, right at the bottom of the pecking order, and be grateful for it.'

'I said nothing of the sort!'

'Then what else is your objection, Mr Mayhew, to your friend's attentions towards me?'

'Which you encourage,' he snapped back.

'Which I did not encourage, which I did my best to discourage, if you must know. And don't change the subject when the argument begins to go against you.'

'Has no-one ever told you how

impossible you are, Elinor Owen?'

'Frequently.' A spurt of wickedness shot up inside her like fire. 'Which is why Peter's appreciation of me made such a pleasant change.'

'Now you are laughing at me.'

'Ah, so your dignity allowed you to notice, did it?'

'Let me tell you, miss, sarcasm does not become you.'

'And why should I care what you think?'

'Why? Why, you little minx. I thought that must be obvious, even to you.'

Eli opened her mouth to shoot back a reply, and stopped, the sarcasm stilled on her lips.

'What did you just say?'

'I'm not going to repeat it for your amusement, thank you very much,' he retorted.

'Am I laughing?'

She saw a slow smile dawn on his lips.

'Not that I can see.'

'Well, then. You must have said

something right,' she said softly. 'For a change,' she added on a sharper note, as he drew dangerously close, but Richard was not about to rise to her bait again so soon.

'They say practice makes perfect,' he murmured into her hair.

'I'm not sure I like the sound of that,' she replied.

Her legs were beginning to shake uncontrollably, and there was a ringing in her head.

'That sounds like an excuse to behave badly.'

'Do I need an excuse?'

His eyes were dark, and warm, and burning with an intensity that made her insides finally go to pieces, and he bent to meet her lips. She placed a hand impatiently over his mouth.

'Richard, not now! Listen!'

From down below there floated up towards them the sound of angry voices.

'What is the meaning of this?'

It was Lady Sara, loud and furious, but Eli could hear just the faintest touch of fear in her voice.

'Nothing, dear lady. A little, shall we say, invasion, that is all. It seemed from the panic in your servants that you were missing one of your household.'

Eli held Richard tight, preventing him from rushing down to confront Jacques there and then.

'A highly-valued member of your household. I take it you recognise this so-lovely bonnet,' Jacques was now saying.

'I see.' Sara's voice was hard, and cold. 'I take it you have come to bargain.'

'Of course, dear lady, in which I shall have the worst of the deal.'

'You surprise me.'

'But, dear lady, what is a small, insignificant piece of gravel compared to a most precious life?'

'Don't!' Eli hissed, pulling Richard back towards the panelling behind them. 'Think, Richard, if you go down there now you'll be as helpless as the rest of them.'

From below, there came the steady tread of footsteps. Jacques, it seemed, had come prepared this time.

'He's got a small army with him. Hurry, this is the only chance to help Sara, and your sister.'

The heavy tread had stopped.

'Search the house. I want everyone within these walls down in this hallway instantly.'

The moment Jacques' voice stopped there was a rapid thud of boots towards the stairs.

'Come on,' Eli urged. 'The secret passageways. They have to at least give us a chance!'

To her relief, she saw Richard nod. The next moment he had grasped her hand and was racing up with her to the next floor.

'The tapestry,' he hissed.

They shot behind a large, worked piece depicting a dead King Arthur being rowed over Snowdon's lake to the cave beneath its summit. The footsteps were now pounding up the stairs, drawing even closer.

'It has to be here somewhere.'

He felt amongst the panels for the hidden lever.

'Hurry!' Eli urged.

She could make out the shadow of the first ruffian as he reached the top of the staircase. In a moment they would be surrounded.

'Got it!'

Richard pulled the lever, and the next moment they were inside the panelling, securing the secret door back into place. They both leaned against the wood, holding their breath. Had they been spotted vanishing?

Eli shut her eyes, expecting axes to beat down their wooden protection at any moment. But, instead, all she could hear was a voice shouting out orders in rapid succession, and footsteps vanishing in all directions.

She opened her eyes to meet Richard's smile of relief. They had made it! His arms came around her, holding her tight.

'All right,' he whispered softly, 'let's get going. We've a rescue to complete.'

9

Quickly,' Richard whispered urgently. 'We have no time to lose. They could decide to search this room at any moment.'

He helped Peter swing down from his makeshift bed, and limp out of the dressing-room, across Lady Sara's bedroom, towards the secret door hidden behind a large tapestry of King Arthur taking his sword, Excalibur, from the Lady of the Lake, with Snowdon rising up behind, and a very long-bearded and solemn Merlin looking on.

'Eli?'

He turned back. She was not following.

'You go ahead. I'll clear up here as best I can. We don't want to leave any evidence to let them know Peter was here,' she whispered.

'It's not safe.'

'If they find me, they'll only find a housemaid and put me with the other servants, while if they find you . . . '

Richard hesitated, but the rapid march of feet was reaching Lady Sara's bedroom. With a brief nod, he impelled Peter towards the door in the panelling, shutting it quickly behind them.

Eli worked fast, removing any evidence she could find of the invalid and bundling the sheets and blankets from the makeshift bed into the large laundry basket in one corner. She gave one last look around. Good, there was nothing there that did not look out of place in a lady's dressing-room. Now all she had to do was to negotiate safely the short space between the dressing-room and the secret opening. She had taken only a few steps when the door of the bedroom was swung open abruptly.

'After you, dear lady,' an unpleasantly familiar voice came.

Eli froze. In a moment they would be between her and the safety of the secret passageway, and she had no illusions that Jacques would not take the precaution of searching Sara's room. Quick as a flash, she ran back into the dressing-room and climbed into the laundry basket, pulling the dirty sheets and blankets over her as much as she could. Then she crouched there, heart hammering.

'And what are you expecting to find? Assassins?' Sara's acid tones came.

Eli held her breath. Several of Jacques' men appeared to have followed him inside the room, and were now engaged in a thorough inspection of every nook and cranny. She heard cupboards being opened, and furniture moved.

'I don't know what you think can possibly be hiding in there,' Lady Raglan remarked. 'I'm not in the habit of employing fairy people. Come to that, rumour is they left here when King Arthur went to Avalon.'

'So entertaining, dear Lady,' Jacques murmured, 'under the most adverse of circumstances. And in there,' he added sharply to some henchman or other. 'Remarkable what can be hidden in a lady's dressing-room.'

'And you would have experience of this, I suppose,' Sara said coldly.

'Of course.' There was a definite smirk in his voice. 'You are not the only lady of my acquaintance to welcome me into her private rooms.'

'We are all young and foolish once,' she snapped in return.

Eli crouched as low as she could, without daring to breathe. She heard the tread of feet, the creak of the bed as it was moved, and the swish of Lady Sara's dresses. Light shone in on her as the basket lid was lifted.

'Anything?'

Jacques was growing impatient. The searcher was distracted and the laundry basket lid was dropped back into place.

'Nothing, sir. Just the usual.'

'Lost something, have you? How very careless,' Sara remarked acidly.

'It can keep.'

It appeared Jacques had decided he

was wasting his time.

'Without the Eagle Stone, what is he? A playboy, without the means of playing, unless his cousin, the Queen, gives him a place at her court, which I doubt. Her Majesty is not in the habit of wasting money, so I've heard. All right, you can go. I want two of you posted outside this room. No-one is to go in or out without my say-so.'

The footsteps left the room, and Eli could at least breathe more easily.

'I told you there was nothing here.'

Sara's voice was even. At least, Eli thought, she would know that someone had escaped Jacques' rounding-up of the household and helped Peter to escape. At least she would have that hope to cling to.

'All right. You've made your point.'

No more smooth tones from Jacques. It seemed the gloves were off.

'Now, Sara, no more games, not if you want to see your niece alive again. Where is the Eagle Stone?'

'I don't have it with me here. Surely

you must have realised that when you searched my house earlier.'

'You're bluffing. There are endless hiding places here. Smuggling, wasn't that the true source of the Raglan wealth? The old man, at least, believed it. Looking for some old passageway beneath the house, wasn't he?'

Eli froze, her breath coming short and fast. So Jacques had heard of the passageway, maybe even already found it.

'He was mad. Haven't you heard? It's still the talk of the village,' Sara pointed out.

'Not nearly as mad as he would have you believe. You forget I knew him, Sara. He was eccentric, certainly, but insane? I very much doubt it. Simply a means of behaving as badly as he pleased. You should try it some time.'

'As if I would take any suggestion of yours.'

This was followed by a moment's silence.

'You were happy enough to learn

from me, once,' he replied then, his voice softening to a more gentle tone.

'When I was too young to know any better. I have grown wiser since.'

'Sara, Sara, why should we fight like this? All I am asking for is a stone, a simple stone, a symbol with no other worth. Why must you fight battles that are not yours? I have no wish to harm you, or your family. Why must we be on opposite sides? We were good together. Why should we not be so again?'

'You expect me to betray my friends?' she demanded.

'Your friends!' He gave a contemptuous snort. 'Do you think the royal family of Milat has any interest in you, beyond being a useful servant? They are scarcely rushing to your aid now.'

'Must you always believe the worst of people?'

'And must you always believe the best, against all evidence?'

'That I do not, not any more. You cured me of that, Jacques. I did believe in you. I loved you. I'd have been quite content to spend the rest of my life as a fencing master's wife, even though my family never spoke to me again. But you wanted more, always more. Was it just the Raglan wealth you were after, after all?'

'Of course not, Sara. It was you I wanted. Your family's money meant nothing to me.'

'But money did, Jacques, and soon you didn't care where it came from. Why do you think I left you?'

'You preferred to live with some desert savage in a tent!' he returned, bitterly.

'Sheik el Marrak was no savage,' Sara said angrily. 'He was a good man, a cultured man, who fought to preserve the heritage of his people. I loved him until the day he died. He would never have become a mercenary, fighting simply for the highest-paying master, whoever they might be.'

'Well, you have made your choice,' Jacques said with a sneer. 'And now I hold all the cards. So, what is it to be,

Sara, your niece, or the Eagle Stone?'

'I will show you the Eagle Stone.'

She sounded tired, and defeated.

'Good. I see you have come to your senses at last. Come on then, Lady Raglan, no time like the present.'

'It isn't here.'

'I warned you, no more games.'

'And I told you the Eagle Stone is not here.'

'Where, then?'

'On Snowdon.'

'Liar!'

'Jacques, why should I lie now? As you said, you have all the cards. The stone is hidden on the summit of Snowdon.'

'Where?'

'You'll never find it, even if I explain. That was the general idea,' she added, with a flash of her old spirit.

'Very well, you can show me now.'

'Not today. It is already too late. We would never get up there in the light.'

'Very well, then, first thing tomorrow.'

'On one condition.'

'Condition? My dear Sara, you are hardly in a position to dictate terms.'

'On condition that I see my niece, alive and well, and that she stays in this house while we are gone. It's in your own best interest, Jacques. If I am not entirely convinced that Catherine will be alive when I come down, I might just be tempted to throw myself off the top, and take you with me.'

There was a long silence with Jacques clearly mulling this over.

'Very well,' he said at last. 'She will be brought here at dawn, and your nephew, if he returns from this walking trip you tell me he has embarked on, while we are here. My men have surrounded the house. No-one will be able to move in or out without being seen. So no heroics, my dear Sara, please. I should hate to see any of your household harmed.'

'I would never risk it.'

'Mmm,' he returned, sounding unconvinced. 'Until tomorrow then, Sara.

I suggest you get some rest. You will need it.'

Then he was gone, striding out of the door and locking it behind him.

Eli waited a few moments, and then climbed her way out of the linen basket. She found Lady Sara already opening the secret door to the passageway.

'Eli!' she mouthed, and shut the door once more, before following Eli back into the dressing-room, as far away from the soldiers guarding the door as possible. 'Richard and Peter?'

'They're safe.'

'Thank goodness. I take it you heard all that?'

Eli nodded.

'Are you really going to take him on to Snowdon?' she asked Lady Sara.

'Oh, yes. He has left me with no other choice.'

'And the stone?'

'It is up there. I hid it that day we met Jacques. I knew then he would never rest until he got his hands on it. His master pays too well.'

She sighed, and covered her face for a moment.

'Milat has great wealth, you see, gold and silver mines, and a tradition of gold working that goes back for centuries. Peter's father may not have been the best of kings, but at least he loved his country. The military who wish to take over and put their own puppet on the throne are only interested in stripping the land of its treasures, and then leaving its people to their fate. I can't let him do that, Eli.'

'But Catherine . . . '

'Yes. Listen, Eli, the moment I leave with Jacques, you and Richard must find a way of freeing her. Then take Peter and leave, as far away as you can get. Hortense should arrive any moment with soldiers from London, but they may be too late.'

'But if Jacques has the stone . . . ' Eli faltered, suddenly sick to the stomach.

'Do you think he will leave any witnesses? What do you think his orders are, Eli? And if it is a question of money, he will follow those orders to the letter. He knows me well enough to know I would need to see Catherine unharmed before I betray my trust, but after he has the stone, he will have no more use for any of us. You will have a few hours at the most. You must free her, and save yourselves.'

'And you?'

Eli gazed at the stern face in front of her, and her blood ran cold.

'Me? I shall do what I have to do.'

'But Lady Sara!'

Eli stopped, tears in her eyes. She knew instantly that there was nothing she could say to change the older woman's mind.

'Nonsense, my dear, no need to upset yourself.'

Lady Sara was smiling. She patted Eli's cheek gently.

'I have had a good life. I have lived it as I have wanted to live it, despite what anyone said. Now, you had better go. You have work to do, and we can't have any of Jacques' minions finding you here.'

'No, Lady Sara.'

On an impulse, Eli kissed her employer's cheek, and turned towards the main part of the bedroom.

'Eli?'

'Yes, Lady Sara?'

'My nephew. Oh, I'm not so old that I haven't been able to see where the wind blows these past few days, and I rather suspect my nephew needs to marry the woman he loves, whatever anyone might say.'

'Yes, Lady Sara,' Eli said, smiling through her tears.

A few moments later, she was vanishing through the secret doorway and into the safety of the secret passageways.

10

They've put Catherine in her own room,' Eli said quietly, early next morning as she joined Richard at one of the tiny slits of windows, watching Jacques and Lady Sara begin their long trek up the summit of Snowdon, through swirls of white mist.

'Damn. That makes things difficult. It's on the opposite side of the house. The passageways don't go anywhere near it.'

'So what do we do now?' Peter asked, munching a piece of the bread and cheese Eli had managed to steal from the kitchens as she mingled with the other servants that morning in order to follow events with her own eyes.

As she had hoped, none of the guards had taken much notice of which housemaid was which, while the Raglan staff themselves were too terrified by the whole experience to question her sudden reappearance. Only Miriam had begun to ask her where she had been hiding, but Eli had silenced her, and set about pocketing as many provisions as she could find, before taking the first opportunity to creep behind the panelling once more.

'We have to get her out,' Eli said, 'as soon as possible.'

She shuddered, thinking of Lady Sara's words yesterday. Were the guards' instructions even to keep Catherine alive until Jacques returned with the stone? She thought of Miriam and the others, waiting below. Miriam had said Jacques had told the staff it was a simple robbery, and they would soon all be released. She shivered.

How long did they have until the soldiers silenced them all? If only Hortense and Queen Victoria's soldiers had arrived in time! Surely they must be here at any moment, unless Jacques had known all about Lady Sara's ploy all along, and not even Hortense's best disguise had kept her safe.

'Surprise,' Richard said grimly, 'is the only weapon we have, along with these.'

He gestured to the collection of ancient muskets and pikestaffs that looked as if they had not been touched since the Civil War, some two hundred years ago, and were rusted, and half rotted away. Eli eyed them uneasily. What chance did those have against modern rifles and pistols?

'Richard.'

She was aware of Peter clearing his throat, and tactfully turning his back, employing himself busily in cleaning the rusting ends of the pikestaffs.

'I have to do something, however uncertain. I can't just leave her there.'

He met her eyes. Eli swallowed. He believed, as Lady Sara did, that Jacques would be leaving no witnesses to the stealing of the Eagle Stone.

'Then I'm coming with you.'

'No!'

'Peter can hardly walk, and there are two guards outside Catherine's room.'

Along with the rest below, she realised, but she put the thought out of her mind, quickly.

'At least I can get Catherine out of there and to safety.'

Slowly, Richard nodded. Peter or no Peter, he held her tight for a moment, his lips meeting hers.

'All or nothing, eh?' he said, softly.

'All or nothing,' she replied, trying her best to smile. 'Now show me how to use these things.'

'What was that?'

Peter was scrambling to his feet, steadying himself against the wall. Echoing along the passages, the sound came again.

'Gunshot!' Richard had already grasped the most serviceable-looking pikestaff, and was racing off down the passage-way. Without a moment's hesitation, Eli grasped the musket nearest her and was running after him, with Peter limping along behind. The passageway opened into an empty room, a few doors down from Catherine's apartments. Eli emerged into the darkness of the corridor to find a cloud of smoke accompanied by the acrid smell of gunpowder.

'Just put that down quietly, if you please, sir.'

Eli blinked. The smartly-uniformed soldiers bore no resemblance whatsoever to Jacques' motley crew.

'I think the young lady has had enough upset for one day,' the sergeant continued tactfully.

From within the room, Eli could hear the sound of female weeping.

'If my sister has been harmed,' Richard began, but the sergeant lowered his rifle.

'She's quite all right, Mr Mayhew,' he said, relaxing visibly. 'Just a little shocked. Never pleasant for a lady to witness bloodshed.'

Richard pushed past him, and into Catherine's room. The soldier's eyes widened as he took in Eli, ancient musket beneath her arm, and Peter limping behind her, pike at the ready.

'The cavalry, I presume?' he remarked,

with the faintest of grins. 'Good job we got here first. No offence intended, miss,' he added as Eli eyed him anxiously.

'The others? The staff held in the kitchen. Are they all right?'

'Safe and sound, miss. A few bruises, and a good dose of terror, but apart from that, safe and sound.'

His eyes widened as Peter drew closer. Abruptly, he stood to attention.

'Thank goodness you are unharmed, sir,' he said. 'The staff here seemed to be quite unaware of your presence. We were beginning to be afraid.'

'Oh, I was safe enough,' Peter said, 'though of not much help, I'm afraid.'

'We have everyone under lock and key,' the sergeant said. 'Though not, I'm afraid, their leader, as yet.'

'He left an hour or so ago,' Richard said, emerging with Catherine, still weeping gently on his shoulder.

'You wouldn't happen to know where?'

'He's climbing with Lady Raglan to the summit of Snowdon,' Richard said.

'The summit!'

This unexpected information had even the sergeant floored.

'Not a pleasure trip, I take it?'

'No. They are going to fetch the Eagle Stone.'

'Are they, indeed?'

'My sister was being held as a hostage until their return with the stone,' Richard said, frowning. 'Lady Sara had no choice in this.'

'No, sir.' The sergeant was frowning. 'Not like Lady Raglan,' he added, 'to give up without a fight.'

He met Eli's distressed eyes, and his frown deepened.

'Not like her at all. The sooner we have a search party after them, the better. Do you happen to know where the nearest guide can be found, sir?'

'The nearest will be Tam, in the village,' Eli put in, 'but if you go for him, you will waste precious time. In any case, he may well have set off with a party of climbers already. All the guides will be fully employed at this time of year.'

'Then we will have to do without.'

'Up in that wilderness?' Richard frowned at him. 'I've been up there, sergeant. The paths are obscure, and the mountain is vast. Besides, the mist is down today. Once lost in that you will never find your way to the top, let alone down again.'

'Then what do you suggest?'

'I'll be your guide,' Eli said. 'I've been up there often enough. My brother is a guide, and my father works a refreshment hut on the summit. I can find the way for you, even in the mist.'

The sergeant looked dubious.

'I'm sure the young lady means well, and her help is appreciated, but this is a government matter. Besides, the dangers . . . '

'I'm well aware of the dangers!' Eli exclaimed, exasperated. 'If you don't find the correct routes, you'll never get up far enough to face the dangers. I've seen enough bodies brought down of those who thought they could beat the mountain without help. You have a perfectly good guide here who is willing to take her chances. And besides, I wouldn't wish for anything to happen to Lady Sara, and I know she would never let the Eagle Stone fall into the wrong hands, whatever it cost her.'

'Eli's right.' Richard was pale. 'Aunt Sara would never allow Jacques to take the stone, and every moment we argue, we are wasting time. I'll go with Eli, if no-one else will.'

He looked over towards Peter.

'Look after Catherine, will you, until we come back?'

'With pleasure,' Peter said with a smile.

'Good. Well, come on then, sergeant, we've no time to lose.'

★   ★   ★

The mist had thickened as Richard and Eli began to follow the rough track up Snowdon's flanks, towards the summit. The air was cold, drifting in swirls of white all around them. Rocks loomed up out of nowhere, then were lost again. Their faces were damp with water droplets, while their clothes were soon heavy with moisture.

'Good, they're still following,' Richard said, pausing for a moment to look back, to where a line of soldiers, their uniforms hastily replaced by the jackets of ordinary climbers, followed their lead. 'You all right, Eli?'

'Yes,' Eli said.

She smiled, and turned back to concentrate on finding the correct route between the maze of sheep and goat tracks that criss-crossed the mountain. They climbed steadily, pausing every now and again to make sure the soldiers had not lost them in the mist. As they climbed higher, the air grew colder. As they topped the first ridge, a breeze began to stir, swirling the cloud around them.

'Looks as if it's lifting,' Richard said.

'It could clear, now the sun is rising,' Eli replied.

That would make their progress

faster, but it would also speed that of Sara and Jacques above them. The grass in front of them began to glow a brighter green. Boulders appeared above them, and then the ridge of the mountain opposite drifted out of the mist for an instant, before disappearing again.

Above them, blue sky began to appear through the cloud. Soon the whiteness was thinning, and the summit of Snowdon swept out of the mist to loom above them. By the time they joined the ridge that would take them to the summit, only wisps were left, sailing down the valleys like ships, and shrouding one peak, and then another, as they swept by. Below them, the lake beside Llanberis gleamed a deep blue, while farther away, there stretched the vast expanse of the sea.

'Look!' Richard exclaimed suddenly. 'There they are!'

Sure enough, right on the very summit, stood two familiar figures.

'They're going to the refreshment

hut,' Eli said. 'No, I'll go,' she added, as Richard began to make his way towards Dad's hut. 'Jacques doesn't know me. At least, he doesn't realise I have anything to do with Lady Sara. If he remembers me at all, it will be from the hut. At least I can get some idea of their plans. You'd better stay here for the moment.'

She looked back at the line of men trailing up behind them.

'Make sure the army looks as if it is bent on pleasure, not a training exercise. I'll come back as soon as I know what Lady Sara is planning.'

She walked on up towards the hut as quickly as she dared. Lady Sara was sitting just outside the entrance, sipping tea, with Jacques next to her, his own tea forgotten in his impatience.

'Well?' he was demanding, as Eli approached.

'I told you. I need to rest, and collect my thoughts.'

'Play for time, more like. I know you, Sara. Well, I won't be fobbed off any more.'

He paused as Eli passed them. He looked up briefly, but without any signs of recognition. Eli took a deep breath.

'Another cup of tea, madam?' she murmured, taking care for her English to sound as hesitant as possible. 'Some of my dad's Bara Brith?'

'No, she does not,' Jacques snapped irritably. 'Go and sell your wares elsewhere.'

'Thank you, Miss Owen.'

It was as if Lady Sara had not heard him. She gazed into Eli's face without expression, but with a sudden light in her eyes.

'Another cup of tea would do nicely.'

Eli nodded, and shot into the hut. Dad looked up as she entered, astonishment at her sudden appearance on his face. Eli put her fingers to her lips to still his exclamation and listened to the two just outside.

'I said, no more games, Sara.'

'And I need another cup of tea, especially before tackling Crib Goch.'

'Crib Goch? What is this Crib Goch?

We are on the summit, are we not?'

'Well, the stone is on Crib Goch, over there.'

'That ridge?' Jacques was contemptuous. 'Why it is almost flat. Why did you not take us there in the first place?'

'There's time enough when I've finished my tea,' Sara said stubbornly.

Eli winced. Jacques might be dismissive, but he hadn't seen Crib Goch close up. The ridge might look harmless from here, but Eli had seen the sheer terror in those reckless, or foolish enough, to allow their guides to take them over the narrow ridge, no more than a footstep wide in places, with a sheer drop on either side to a terrifying distance far below. Heaven knows what Lady Sara was planning. Eli had no desire to think about it too closely. With a quick smile at Dad, she took a cup of tea outside.

'Madam,' she murmured once more.

'Thank you,' Sara replied in Welsh, smiling. 'My niece?' she asked, in casual tones.

'Safe,' Eli replied, trying to sound

equally distant and polite. 'I've brought help.'

'Good,' Sara said, relapsing into English once more. 'I'm glad to hear it, my dear. Your mother is a good woman.'

'Madam,' Eli replied, with a bob of a curtsey.

From the corner of her eye, she saw Jacques frowning impatiently, with no signs of finding anything suspicious in this brief exchange. She picked up an empty jug from outside the door, and walked slowly in the direction of Blod, chewing hay a little way from the hut, as if her only intention in life was to fetch more water. The moment she was back over the brow of the ridge and out of sight she took to her heels as fast as she could.

'Well?' Richard demanded, as she arrived, breathless.

'She's taking him over Crib Goch.'

'Crib Goch?' Richard stared. 'What on earth is she taking him there for?'

'He'll have no way out,' Eli replied.

'The ridge is treacherous,' she explained to the waiting sergeant. 'Once on it, there is no way down, except to follow the path, and that is a slow journey. If you post some of your men at this end, and send the rest along the path by the lake to the other descent, there is no way he can escape. The lakeside path is quick and easy. They'll arrive before him without any trouble.'

The sergeant nodded, dispatching his men quickly. The detachment sent to the far end of Crib Goch had already disappeared, and were descending rapidly towards the lake by the time Jacques and Lady Sara finally emerged from the shelter of the refreshment hut, and began to make their way towards Crib Goch, Lady Sara sporting a mild limp as she went, in a clear effort to slow their progress.

'He'll know she planned this,' Richard said. 'The moment he is on that ridge and sees what it is like, he'll know that she planned this. And that if help hadn't come . . . '

'She would have thrown both of them from the highest place,' Eli finished quietly.

'And he won't let her escape that easily,' Richard said.

He grasped her hand, hard. They looked at each other. They both knew they couldn't just leave Sara, not when Jacques, with his plans foiled and arrest imminent, would know he would be facing certain execution as a spy, and had nothing to lose.

The next moment, they were hurrying as fast as they could in the wake of the soldiers already quietly closing ranks behind the two as they reached the perilous rocks of Crib Goch.

11

Eli and Richard reached the ridge just as Lady Sara and Jacques began to emerge on to the path.

'What is it now?' they heard Jacques demand, impatiently.

'I have a stone in my boot. That is what is troubling me. I need to remove it.'

Sara sat down with no signs of moving again.

'You go ahead.'

'Oh, not without you, my dear,' he replied. 'No more delays.'

'As you wish.'

Sara shrugged and rose to her feet with maddening slowness, but, Eli saw, she had achieved her purpose. Jacques, quite unaware of the narrowness of the path ahead, and impatient to quicken the pace, had already stepped on to the ridge. Cloud billowed up around him, obscuring him from view for a moment.

By the time it had cleared again, he was several steps along the path.

'Sara?' Eli heard him call, for once, a little uncertain of himself.

'Right behind you!'

There was a hard edge to Lady Raglan's tone.

'Sara!'

Fury was replacing the momentary fear. Abruptly, the cloud lifted and Eli saw him stumble in sheer surprise, as ground suddenly vanished on either side of him, leaving him stranded on a narrow piece of rock.

'Witch!' he yelled, swaying dangerously on the narrow ledge before recovering himself.

'Never did like heights, did you, Jacques?' Sara called.

She was standing in the shelter of the rocks, looking down at the view of the valley deep below, with excitement on her face.

'Always liked to take risks with other people, never with yourself. Not your body, or your heart. Look into the depths now, Jacques, if you dare.'

'You were going to kill me!'

He seemed strangely outraged at the thought.

'Both of us, if you must know.'

'Lost your courage then, have you, Sara? Or thinking of that pretty little niece of yours?'

'Catherine is quite safe,' she replied, 'and as for killing you, well, Jacques, there is no longer any need.'

Jacques swayed again as he turned himself swiftly, first to the group of men waiting for him at the start of the path, and then to the military march of the group making their way below him beside the lake, making to the other end of the ridge.

'There is no way out,' Sara called, 'unless you would care to jump.'

He yelled, in fury, twisting himself round again. Eli saw the swift movement of his hand inside his jacket. She screamed a warning with all her might but she was already too late. The roar of a pistol filled the still air.

'Eli.'

She felt Richard's arms come around her and hold her tight.

'Eli, don't cry. It's all right.'

'I've never seen anyone die before,' she wept, 'not in front of me like that.'

'I know,' he murmured, brushing the tears away with a gentle hand. 'But it's all over now.'

'And I'm still deaf,' she complained, with a watery smile.

'Well, I can think of a remedy for that,' he returned, 'but I'm not certain that your father would approve. I think he's had quite enough shocks already for one day.'

'Poor Dad.'

Eli disentangled herself to take another sip of hot tea. Inside the refreshment hut, she could hear Dad clattering about with mugs in prospect of numerous new arrivals, and muttering to himself. A shooting on Crib Goch, and a body lying there for all to see, the unpleasant results of falling from the narrow path. Bad for business that, very bad for business. And the military was roaming all over the place!

Snowdon had never seen the like, not to mention his daughter being escorted back in tears, being held in a very unnecessarily close manner by a young gentleman as well-dressed as royalty, Lady Sara Raglan's nephew, no less. Eli sniffed. Over the last few minutes, while he had brewed the tea, she had seen Dad's face cloud over with a slow realisation that his only daughter appeared to be in imminent danger of being turned into a Raglan. Even if it was only half a Raglan, that was bad enough!

'More tea?'

Dad thrust his head out of the door, the clouds turning to thunder. He had probably just got to the thought of grandchildren, Eli decided, suppressing a sudden desire to giggle.

'No, thank you, Dad,' she replied instead. 'You'd better save it for Queen

Victoria's finest. I'm sure even such a small part of the regiment can drink you dry.'

'Hmph,' Dad said in deep disapproval as the sergeant and his motley band of recruits, clearly not worth a thing to Dad out of uniform, appeared.

'Bad business,' the sergeant said, lowering himself on to the nearest stone bench and shaking his head. 'Bad business indeed.'

'Dead?' Richard asked.

'Oh, yes, no doubt of it. Clean shot, straight through the heart. Quite dead before the fall, I should imagine.'

'Idiot!' Dad clicked his tongue, disapproval deepening even further as a wild figure, grey hair streaming, strode down towards them.

'It was all over. What on earth did he try a stupid thing like that for?'

'Tea?' Dad asked.

'Don't approve, eh, Daniel? Too brutal? Well, if it wasn't for the quick thinking of my nephew here, it would have been me at the bottom of that cliff.'

Sara Raglan settled herself down on the low wall outside the refreshment hut and pushed the loose strands of hair from her face.

'Good job I taught you to shoot straight, eh, Richard?'

'Yes, aunt,' Richard replied with a faint smile.

'You all right, Eli?'

'Yes, ma'am. It was all a bit of a shock, that's all.'

'Always is, seeing someone killed. Hope you never have to witness it again, my dear. In fact, I believe I can wish that for myself, too, after all these years.'

She took Daniel's proffered tea and sipped it, thoughtfully.

'Tam still working as a guide, is he, Daniel?'

'I believe so, Lady Sara,' Dad replied, faintly scandalised at thoughts of where this just might lead.

'Good. Best guide there is.'

She looked around her at the blue sky and the mountain peaks and the hills rolling away beneath her.

'I rather think I shall settle for mountain climbing in my old age. A far more civilised pastime, don't you think?'

'And the Eagle Stone?' Eli ventured.

'Ah, the Eagle Stone.'

Sara Raglan smiled and bent down to reach into the stones beneath her.

'It wasn't only that I wished to speak to you, Miss Elinor, that day up here.'

There was a moment's silence as she struggled with something hidden deep inside the low wall. Then she brought out a grubby-looking piece of cloth wrapped tightly round a hard object, roughly the size of a hen's egg. She brushed it with her hand and the cloth fell away, leaving the deep luminescence of the largest emerald Eli had ever seen, even in picture books telling of fantastic stories.

'And there it was, you see, all along. Now the true heir to Milat can take his father's place and set about restoring order once more.'

She gave a brief shudder.

'And after all it has cost, the sooner it is out of my hands and in those of its rightful owner, the better,' she said.

★　★　★

Eli leaned back in the warm sun and watched the little procession begin its way back down towards Llanberis, led by the tall figure of Lady Raglan who seemed to have gained a new lease of life and had soon left her protecting soldiers behind.

'I wish I could stay here for ever,' she murmured as she felt Richard's arms come around her.

'Really?' he murmured in her ear. 'Not exactly what I had in mind.'

'And what exactly was that, Mr Mayhew?'

'Well, I'd love to demonstrate, Miss Owen, but I think the poor climbers of Snowdon would never live it down.'

Eli giggled.

'I'm surprised you think you still

have the energy, after the past few days,' she replied saucily.

'Oh, energy will never be a problem, not with you, Eli.'

He stopped and pulled her round to face him.

'My aunt is proposing that I should learn to take over the Raglan estate, since it will fall to me eventually. I wasn't at all sure at first about leaving London and everything I have there.'

'And now?'

'Now I have no doubts. At this moment, here with you, I can't imagine being happy anywhere else, unless you would rather take up Peter's offer and transform into a princess, that is?'

'I always wanted to be a princess.'

'Eli! You are supposed to answer no, and then kiss me to prove it!'

'That was when I was a child,' she continued, 'but I think I might just give up the idea now. Besides, I think Catherine would make a far prettier royal bride.'

'I hope not,' he replied. 'I can't

imagine Milat being a secure country for a while, Eagle Stone, or no Eagle Stone.'

'I think you are supposed to say that no-one could ever be prettier than me, and then kiss me to prove it,' she retorted and he laughed.

'Do I need to prove it?'

'No,' Eli said with a smile. 'But I thought it might be rather nice.'

'Ah, well, in that case, and if you insist.'

'I most certainly do.'

'And even though your father might well call me out for pistols at dawn?'

'I would do my best to persuade him not to.'

'Well, then, Eli, my love, your wish is my command, as it always will be.'

And, startled climbers or no startled climbers, he enveloped her completely in his warm embrace.

We do hope that you have enjoyed reading this large print book.

Did you know that all of our titles are available for purchase?

We publish a wide range of high quality large print books including:
Romances, Mysteries, Classics
General Fiction
Non Fiction and Westerns

Special interest titles available in large print are:
The Little Oxford Dictionary
Music Book, Song Book
Hymn Book, Service Book

Also available from us courtesy of Oxford University Press:
Young Readers' Dictionary
(large print edition)
Young Readers' Thesaurus
(large print edition)

For further information or a free brochure, please contact us at:
Ulverscroft Large Print Books Ltd.,
The Green, Bradgate Road, Anstey,
Leicester, LE7 7FU, England.
Tel: (00 44) **0116 236 4325**
Fax: (00 44) **0116 234 0205**

*Other titles in the
Linford Romance Library:*

THE FOOLISH HEART

Patricia Robins

Mary Bradbourne's aunt brought her up after her parents died. When she was ten, her aunt had a son, Jackie, who was left with a mental disability as the result of an accident. Unselfish and affectionate, Mary dedicated her life to caring for him. But when she meets Dr. Paul Deal and falls in love with him she faces a dilemma. How will she be able to care for her cousin, when she knows she must follow her heart?

HEIRS TO LOVING

Rachel Ford

When Jenni Green went to trace her father's family in Brittany, she didn't know that she would keep running into Raoul Kerouac, known to everyone in the area as 'Monsieur Raoul'. Autocratically he organises a job for her in the local campsite, and pushes the *gendarmerie* to find Jenni's stolen handbag. Luckily they find it; unluckily Raoul sees it first — for the documents show that Jenni's real name is Eugénie Aimée Kerouac, part owner of the estate . . .